Protecting Summer

Protecting Summer

SEAL of Protection
Book 4

By Susan Stoker

Table of Contents

Chapter One

SAM "MOZART" REED fingered his scarred cheek as he drove his old battered truck toward Big Bear Lake. He'd only told his friend and Navy SEAL teammate, Cookie, where he was going. It wasn't as if he was keeping it a secret from the rest of the team, but he'd been on so many of these "leads" in the past, he'd learned to keep them close to his chest in case it turned out to be nothing.

The good part about being on such a close-knit team was that Mozart knew if he asked for help, all five of his friends would drop whatever it was they were doing to come and assist him. Hell, they probably already had a very good idea of where he was.

And this could very well be a wild-goose-chase, just as most of the other leads Mozart had recently followed up on, but he couldn't blow it off. He'd spend every spare minute he had on any lead, no matter how crazy, because it might, just might, lead him to Ben Hurst.

Mozart had been fifteen years old when his little sister, Avery, was kidnapped. His entire neighborhood in their small town in California had acted quickly and search parties were set up. It'd been an excruciating long seventeen days. Every day had been full of searches and television appearances. His parents had begged and pleaded with whomever had taken Avery to bring her back.

In the end, it'd been a couple hiking in the woods two hundred miles away that found Avery's body. They'd been on a scavenger hunt and had almost tripped over her remains, naked and dumped in the dense forest as if she was trash.

Mozart would never forget the day his parents had heard the news. He'd never seen his dad cry before, but that day he'd bawled. His little baby girl had been violated and murdered. It wasn't something a fifteen-year-old boy could ever forget. His parents were never the same after that and divorced, as many parents of missing and murdered children did, because of the strain. Mozart's dad had passed away a few years later and his mom remarried a man with a ton of money. He didn't see her much anymore, she was too busy gallivanting around the world, trying to forget she ever had a daughter, and definitely not caring her only son was still alive.

The cops had never found the person who'd killed his sister. They were pretty sure they knew who'd done it though. A drifter named Ben Hurst had been traced to their area at the same time Avery had been nabbed. Hurst was a survivalist-type guy who was just as comfortable living off the land as he was living in the middle of a big city. He was big, about six feet tall and weighed about two hundred and fifty pounds. It would've been easy for him to overpower Avery, hell, any child. Hurst was a nasty man who'd spent time in jail for molesting children and for assaulting several different people, and showed no signs of rehabilitation after each of his stints behind bars. It wasn't a stretch to believe Hurst had seen Avery walking home from school and snatched her right off the street. The problem was, the cops couldn't prove it.

Hurst never cooperated with the investigation, of course, and as the years went by, other cases took precedence for the police department. Mozart would never stop searching, however. He'd taken one look at the face on the booking photo he'd seen and memorized it. Mozart vowed to avenge Avery one way or another and he'd made it his goal in life to catch Ben Hurst and make him pay.

Mozart had joined the Navy right out of high school with the specific goal of becoming a Navy SEAL. All his life he'd watched movies and TV shows about the SEALs. They were the best of the best, and the toughest men he'd ever seen. Mozart knew that was what he needed to become if he was going to catch Hurst and make him pay for what he'd done to his baby sister.

His dad might not be alive to see justice served, and Mozart had no idea if his mom would even care anymore, but he couldn't let it go. Mozart had stood next to his sister's tiny little coffin and swore to her that he'd never rest until her killer was behind bars or dead. Even as a teenager, Mozart hadn't backed away from the thought of being the one to kill whomever had murdered Avery. He'd spent the past nineteen years trying to fulfill that promise. It was hard-wired into him now. Nothing and no one would prevent him from following through.

Mozart thought back to the last Christmas he had with his little sister. Avery had been so excited. She'd woken him up way too early and they'd gone downstairs and sat in front of the Christmas tree, presents piled up around it. She'd insisted on "sorting" the presents, even though Mozart had warned her their mom would be pissed.

Mom *had* been mad, but Mozart talked her down and he'd watched with pleasure as Avery exclaimed over her presents. She was the type of kid who appreciated every single thing she'd been given. The cheesy stuffed bear that Mozart had given her had received the same praise as a cheap bracelet set given to her by their neighbor. Mozart had loved Avery with every fiber of his being. She was innocent and precious. Losing her had nearly killed him. He'd barely graduated from high school; his grades had fallen drastically after her death. Life had no meaning, until he'd graduated from BUD/S and made it his mission in life to find Ben Hurst.

Mozart would use his leave to follow up on any lead he'd get to try to track Hurst down. Tex, their computer hacker friend in Virginia, had been monitoring the internet and his computer network for any mention of the man. It was pure chance that Hurst had possibly been seen in Big Bear Lake in California. Big Bear wasn't that far from Riverton, down by San Diego, and Mozart had a week of leave coming to him. They'd been on some intense missions recently. Not to mention, Caroline and Wolf had just gotten married and were on their honeymoon. Commander Hurt had given the whole team the week off, and they'd all been thrilled. Some *real* time off, with no chance of being called in for a mission at a moment's notice. Mozart knew, however, that if the CO knew exactly what he was doing on his time off, he most likely wouldn't be thrilled, so Mozart had kept his mission of revenge to himself.

Mozart thought about his SEAL team buddies as he continued his drive up to Big Bear. He smiled when he thought about Wolf and Ice. Ice, also known as Caroline, was a tough as nails chemist who'd almost single-handedly foiled a terrorist attack on the plane that he,

Wolf, and Abe had been traveling in. If it hadn't been for her, they all would've been dead. That alone made her precious to Mozart.

Mozart was pleased as he could be that Wolf had finally stepped up to the plate and had asked Caroline to marry him. The wedding had gone as wrong as a wedding could go when the limo the men were traveling in to the church was sideswiped by a car that had run a red light. Caroline never faltered though. After hearing that Cookie had been hurt, she, Fiona, and Alabama showed up at the hospital in all their wedding frippery. After making sure Cookie was going to be all right, and the rest of the team was as well, Caroline revealed that she'd offered the pastor a sizeable donation if she'd come to the hospital to marry her and Wolf.

And that's what they'd done. Wolf and Ice stood by Cookie's hospital bed, surrounded by their friends and pledged to love each other for the rest of their lives. Mozart would never admit it, even if tortured, but it was one of the most beautiful things he'd ever seen. Ice was a hell of a woman, and he was thrilled Wolf had found someone to complete him.

Mozart didn't think he'd ever settle down with one woman though. He was the flirt of the team. Mozart couldn't remember most of the women's names he'd hooked up with over the years. Time and time again he'd gone home with some woman from a bar, then left as soon as they'd had sex. That was all it was to him. Sex. Mozart never bothered to "date" a woman, he didn't need to.

Unfortunately, the terrorists that kidnapped Caroline in Virginia carved up Mozart's face pretty good. Knowing it made him sound like an asshole, but not caring, Mozart figured if a woman didn't want to have sex with him because of his face, he frankly didn't care. At least five more women were behind that one that would love to suck him off or spend a night in his bed. Being a SEAL was good for his sex life, nasty facial scars or not. His scars didn't bother Mozart. He'd been through a lot worse in his life; scars on his face were the least of his worries. Losing his sister to a psychopath was bad. Scars on his face? He didn't care.

Mozart was aware women found him good-looking. When he was younger he'd taken advantage of that, but now it was what it was. He was muscular, as was everyone on his team. He had dark hair that was just a shade too long to be considered appropriate for the military. A woman once told him he had high cheekbones and dark eyes that seemed to be able to look right into a woman's soul and pull out her deepest desires. It was all bullshit to Mozart, but since his looks helped him get laid, he'd cultivated it.

Now, with his once rugged face split by three deep scars on the right side, he had to rely more on his personality to find a woman who would sleep with him. Mozart knew on some level Ice felt guilty about what had happened to his face. He'd told her every time she brought it up that it hadn't been her fault, and at last, she'd stopped apologizing to him. Mozart was honest when he told Ice he was okay with his face, because he was. He was old enough now, thirty-four, to know he'd escaped death too many times to take life for granted.

He was tall, about six four, and he generally towered over most people. That, coupled with his dark intense look, had been good for intimidating bad guys and for making women feel small and cherished, even if it was only for a night. And it was *always* only for a night.

Thinking back to his team, Mozart recalled how Abe had been the next team member to find a woman after Wolf claimed Ice. Abe and Alabama had been together for a while now. Abe had almost screwed it up with her though. Alabama tried to project a tough image, but Mozart, and Abe, had seen right through it. She was currently taking classes at the local community college to see what it was she wanted to do with her life, but for now, she and Abe were disgustingly happy.

Cookie and Fiona were also pretty darn happy, but for Fiona it'd been a long hard road. They'd all met Fiona in Mexico where they'd saved her from a sex-slave ring. She'd been violated and the kidnappers had hooked her on some serious drugs. The women in

Mozart's teammates' lives certainly had the market on strength. They'd all been through some horrific things, but somehow, with the help of their SEAL men, and some professional help, had come through all right.

Mozart smiled, thinking about how close all the women were. When the team was called away on a mission they all spent time together supporting each other. Nothing made their men feel better than to know their women had a support system while they were off fighting for their country. Mozart might pretend to be annoyed at the guys for being so attached to their women, but if he was honest, deep down, a part of him was jealous.

Mozart had always looked out for others. He'd always been the guy people called when they needed help. He was the flirt, the laid back good-time guy. The guy to take home for a night then left in search of another conquest. Mozart had never known what it was to be wanted for who you were, not for what you could do for someone, or what job you had.

Mozart shook his head in disgust. Whatever. In the end, it didn't matter. He just had to get up to the lake and see if he could find the person that may or may not be Hurst. Once he found him, and either killed him or turned him over to the authorities, he'd see what he could do about possibly getting a long-term girlfriend. Being around Ice, Alabama, and Fiona had made

Mozart see, for the first time, that having someone to love might not be the horrible thing he'd always thought it was. Of course, he'd have to find someone as perfect as his teammates' women, and that would be a pretty tough task.

Mozart pulled into the parking lot of *Big Bear Lake Cabins* and cut off his ignition. Looking at the place, he could only shake his head. He'd made the reservation online. It was cheap and looked clean enough on the few pictures that had been showcased on the travel site. In reality, it was pretty run down and the cabins looked like they'd fall down with one hard storm.

There were twelve separate small buildings, each within about five feet of each other. Some had small porches and others just had an overhang over the door. The paint was peeling off most of the buildings, and Mozart could see that most of the roofs on the buildings needed some sort of repair.

Mozart noticed a maid's cart in front of one of the cabins on the far side. He had the mean thought that the maid was probably as run-down as the cabins themselves, but dismissed even thinking about the person that cleaned the crappy motel for a living. There was a small building with a sign that read "Office" off to his right, and next to that what looked like an outhouse. The only reason Mozart knew it wasn't a restroom was because of the sign on the door that announced it was for storage.

Mozart absently fingered the scar on the right side of his face again, he'd noticed he'd started doing that when he was deep in thought, and turned his mind to what his first steps were in trying to track Hurst down. Mozart didn't care where he slept; he'd certainly slept in worse conditions on most of the team's missions. Mozart would have moved on and found a different place, but justified staying because he just needed a place to keep his stuff and to sleep each night. If it was clean, it was only a bonus.

Mozart exited his truck and headed toward the office. It was time to hunt down a child-molesting killer.

Chapter Two

SUMMER, KNEELING BY the cleaning cart, stood up slowly and heard her knees creak in protest. She ignored the sound, grabbed a stack of towels, and headed into the little cabin she was currently cleaning. The job was monotonous and boring as hell, but it was a job and it allowed her the freedom to just...be. She'd needed it after the hellacious year she'd had. Cleaning hotel rooms wasn't what she'd envisioned for her life, but for now, she didn't want to be anywhere else. It was easy and comfortable and she could be anonymous. She couldn't handle anything else right now.

Summer thought back on her life. She used to *be* somebody. She had her Master's Degree in Human Resources and worked at a Fortune 500 company in Phoenix, Arizona. She was married and had a good salary, lived in a nice house, and had a perfect life. That life came crumbling down like a house of cards and Summer still wasn't sure how it happened. She'd come home from work one day and her husband was gone.

Just gone. All his stuff in the house moved out. There was a note on the kitchen counter that explained he wasn't happy and had met another woman. He didn't want to hurt Summer, but he didn't love her anymore and he thought their life was a sham. Summer had been blindsided. Sure, she knew there wasn't much passion in their relationship, but they were comfortable. Maybe that was the problem. They were too comfortable. Summer signed the divorce papers without contesting them when they'd arrived in the mail later that year. There was no point in protesting.

It wasn't too long after she'd been officially divorced, that she learned her company was downsizing and she lost her job. She'd tried to find another position, with no luck. It seemed as if no one wanted to hire a thirty-six year old woman with only HR experience. They wanted to hire new graduates with no master's degree so they could pay them less than her experience and education would warrant. Summer soon couldn't pay her mortgage and lost the house.

Summer knew she was an introvert. Sure, she could socialize with anyone, but she had a hard time making lifelong friends. All her life she'd met people, but not one took the extra effort to keep in touch once she moved away. Not high school friends, not college friends, not friends from work. Summer wasn't sure what it was about her that made people not want to form close attachments that would survive a long-distance relationship. Losing her job was no different. All of her coworkers were very sympathetic and made all sorts of offers to get together for lunch and nights out, but not one of them followed through. Summer was used to it.

She made friends easily enough, but they weren't the kind of friends Summer saw on television and read about in books. They weren't life-long friends who she could call up for a girls-night-out or crash at one of their houses temporarily.

One day she'd had enough. She'd been living in a crappy apartment where she didn't feel safe and didn't have any job prospects on the horizon. Summer packed up what was important to her, and just left. She drove her piece of crap car until it too died on her. She used the last of her money to get a bus ticket to the little town of Big Bear in the mountains of California.

Summer had seen the little motel called *Big Bear Lake Cabins* one day, and miraculously there was a "Help Wanted" sign in the office window. The owner wasn't very friendly, but apparently, he was desperate, because he told her she had the job.

So here she was. No car. No money. All of her belongings fit into one suitcase. She was pathetic, but she was also free. No mortgage, no expectations. She had nothing, she was nobody. And for now it was heaven.

When she'd arrived with her suitcase in hand, Henry, the owner of the cabins, had been blunt with her.

"I don't have any open cabins you can live in, but if you really need a place to stay, you can sleep in the building next to the office."

"The storage building?" Summer had asked incredulously, looking askance at the tiny building that looked like it could hold a maid's cart, and little else.

"Yup. There's no kitchen or bathroom, but there's a small shower and toilet in the back of the office that you can use."

Summer had taken a deep breath and almost told Henry where he could shove his pathetic motel and his not-so-generous housing offer, but she bit her lip and meekly nodded. She really didn't have a choice.

When Summer opened the storage building she saw that it did have a small sink, she was vastly relieved to know there was at least some running water in her new "home." The sink was used mostly to fill the mop bucket, but it didn't matter. Water was water. The building had no heat or no air conditioning, which in the summer months wasn't a huge deal because it rarely got sweltering hot up in the mountains. Winter would be a bit dicier, but Summer figured she'd worry about that when the time came. Maybe by then she'd have earned enough money to move into a real apartment and it'd be a moot point. The little storage shack wasn't very sturdy, but Summer knew that beggars couldn't be choosers.

Her bed was a cot up against the wall. Henry had dug the thing out of some closet somewhere when she'd asked where she was supposed to sleep. It was missing one foot so it sat lop-sided and swayed precariously when she sat or lay down on it. Luckily, it was one of the back feet that was gone, so her head wasn't hanging lower than her feet all night.

Mops, brooms, and shelves that held various cleaning implements and liquids surrounded Summer. It smelled like ammonia and other funky cleaning supplies, but she was thankful for it. She supposed some people would look at her and at her life and turn up their nose or even feel sorry or pity for her, but after living a so-called "perfect" life, and still being miserable, at least now Summer only had to rely on herself. It was liberating.

The only issue had with her new life was that she was always hungry. She wasn't making enough money to be able to buy huge meals, and besides that, she had nowhere to put anything. She had no refrigerator and no stove to cook anything. Henry grudgingly provided breakfast for her, of course subtracting it from her already meager pay, but Summer was on her own for lunch and dinner.

Henry had explained why he served a continental

breakfast to the people staying at the motel. "I sure as hell don't want to, it's wasted money if you ask me, but because of all those fancy-ass hotels and things now, people expect it. They're cheapskates and want more and more for less and less money," he'd complained to her.

Summer had just shook her head. She didn't dare say aloud what she was thinking, namely that Henry himself was the cheapskate.

"Now I have to go shopping every damn week and buy fruit and shit. It's expensive and I hate it. I get granola bars and cereal as well. The guests usually don't stay and chat, they just grab the free breakfast I provide for them and head out to the slopes or to the lake." Henry finally got to the heart of the matter, at least what was important to Summer. "I suppose it'd be okay if you grabbed something each morning as well, but don't go crazy. If I catch you taking more than you can eat and taking advantage of me, I'll change my mind."

"Thank you, Henry. That's very generous of you. I'll just take something small each morning. I won't take advantage."

Henry had just grunted and said in a low voice, "Hope it stays that way."

Even though Summer had promised to only take something small, she usually managed to grab an extra piece of fruit or bread at breakfast that she could snack on during the day. Dinner was usually out of the question. Summer couldn't afford to actually pay to eat at any of the nearby lodges, and she had no transportation, or money, to eat at any of the fast food restaurants in town. So, after cleaning all the cabins, Summer either took a hike around the nearby lake, or she went back to her little cubby hole and tried to ignore her rumbling stomach.

Luckily, it hadn't been too cold, or hadn't been so far, but the warm weather was coming to a close. It was getting colder in the mountains. Henry had told Summer she could keep her job over the winter, but he warned her that she'd make even less money than she did now. They weren't as busy in the winter and he couldn't afford to pay her the full salary he was paying her now. Summer knew it was absurd. He wasn't paying her very much as it was, but she agreed anyway. She figured it'd be a place to stay over the winter if she needed it, and if she felt like leaving, she would. Nothing was tying her here.

For the most part, Summer was satisfied. She was just tired. Tired of merely existing, but she didn't know what to do. This was it for her. This was her life. Yes, she had a master's degree, but it hadn't helped keep her marriage intact, and hadn't helped her keep her job. So be it.

Summer turned away from her cart with an armful

of clean towels and turned, without looking, toward the door to the cabin. She bounced off a hard chest and would have fallen if the man she'd just plowed into hadn't grabbed her elbows and steadied her. Summer looked up and gulped. She was looking at the best looking man she'd ever seen in her life. No lie. The best looking *and* scariest looking. The man was huge. At least a head taller than her five-eight. His arms were big. His hands were big. But the scariest thing about him, was the look on his face. He had a five o'clock shadow that didn't hide the scars that covered the right side of his face. The scars pulled at his mouth and made it look like he was grimacing at her. His hair was dark and a little wild around his head. He was dressed head to toe in black. Each thing, taken separately, wouldn't have worried her, but when Summer took in all of it at once, it was intimidating and actually scared her. But when the man didn't actually do or say anything, just stood there, looking down at her with an incomprehensible look on his face, she got a little pissed. After a few seconds, when he *still* didn't say anything, just continued to keep hold of her elbows and stare down at her, Summer knew she had to do something.

"Uh, sorry, sir," she stammered out. Summer would've backed away from him if she could, but he was still holding on to her elbows where he'd grabbed her to steady her.

Summer expected him to apologize back, or at least respond verbally to her words, but he merely held on to her for a beat more, then let go and took a step back. He nodded at her, then stepped around her and headed toward another cabin that was nearby.

Summer watched him go. She wished she could've heard his voice. She bet it was low and rumbly. His butt was tight and....shit. What was she thinking? Summer whipped around and headed into the cabin she was cleaning. He wasn't for her. No one was anymore. It wasn't easy, but she put the big man out of her head and went back to the monotonous job of straightening up the cabin. If her thoughts strayed back to the man and his delectable ass every now and then, she figured no one would blame her. He was a fine specimen of the male species.

Mozart walked into his cabin and chuckled under his breath at the maid's actions. She'd startled him as she ran right into him as he'd walked past her, but luckily he hadn't knocked her over. He didn't think he'd been walking quietly, and had thought for sure she knew he was there, but obviously he'd been wrong.

Mozart had been surprised at how well the woman fit in his arms. If he'd pulled her into him, her head would've fit right in the crook of his shoulder. Mozart couldn't tell what kind of hair she had, as it was pulled back into a severe looking knot at the back of her head.

Her hair seemed to be a mixture of light colors, but he could also tell she wasn't young. Mozart was surprised to see that she wasn't a college kid earning money while taking classes, but she also wasn't elderly, working because she was bored. If he had to guess, Mozart would say she was probably around his age. Mid-thirties most likely. The *Big Bear Lake Cabins* was the last place he'd have expected to find someone like her.

She was attractive. Mozart admitted it, but didn't like it. He was busy. But she smelled clean, she had laugh lines at the sides of her eyes, of course she'd probably call them crow's feet. The complete package looked good.

Mozart laughed at himself. His thoughts were ridiculous. He'd had seen the look of interest in the woman's eyes, before it'd turned to consternation. He'd seen it time and time again. Women would first think he was good looking, and then once they'd see his scars, they'd be turned off. But now that Mozart thought about it a bit more, the maid hadn't seemed turned off, just startled. Once she'd had a chance to gain her equilibrium, she'd looked him straight in the eyes and even looked as if she was getting pissed at him. It'd been a long time since a woman had bothered to show him any *real* emotion. Mozart was too used to women being fake and doing anything they could to get him into bed. And that pissed look on her face was kinda cute.

Mozart shook his head and tried to put the maid out of his mind. He had to focus on Hurst and on where he might be. As good looking as she'd been, he didn't have time for a roll in the hay. He thought about the information Tex had sent to him before he'd left Riverton. The man believed to be Hurst, was apparently camping out somewhere in the forest surrounding the lake. There'd been reports of petty thefts of small items that Mozart would bet his life had been Hurst. He pulled out the terrain maps of Big Bear and tried to narrow down where the son-of-a-bitch could be holed up. The forest surrounding the area was huge, but Mozart would find him if he was there. Mozart had been trained by the best. Hurst would have no idea he was being stalked until it was too late.

Chapter Three

★

SUMMER TRIED NOT to be aware of the big man in cabin three, but it was hard not to notice him. Every time she cleaned his cabin, she was aware of how good he smelled. She only allowed herself to bury her face into one of his towels once, and felt ashamed after she did it. He didn't know she existed, and that was par for the course. First of all, she was a damn maid, and second he was beautiful, even with his scars. She wasn't. She wasn't putting herself down; she just knew what she was and what she wasn't. In her former life she knew she needed to lose some weight, but that was hard to do with a desk job. But now that she really only ate one meal a day, she'd lost a lot of weight, too much. She figured it wasn't helping her looks any.

The man was extremely neat. All of his clothes were put away in the drawers in the room. His shoes were lined up next to the wall. Any towels that he used were hung up over the shower rod. He'd made his bed every morning. There really wasn't much to clean in his room, but Summer always vacuumed and changed his towels out. She saw him twice at the office. The first time he was eating breakfast and was dressed to go hiking. She saw his backpack against a wall and he was wearing boots, a flannel shirt, and khakis. The second time she saw him was when she knocked on his door to clean his room and he opened the door, nodded at her, and left. She wondered what he was doing here and how long he was staying.

Most of the time when people came to the cabins they were there for a long weekend and almost always with someone else. It was unusual for someone to stay as long as this man had and be by himself. Summer had noticed he went hiking most days, so maybe he just needed the time off of work and wanted to be alone. She mentally shrugged. She had another long day ahead of her. She ignored her rumbling tummy and forced herself to close and lock the cabin door and head for the next room.

MOZART BLEW OUT a breath. It'd been a long day, but a productive one. He'd found evidence that a person had been in the mountains nearby. Mozart figured it had to be Hurst. He was careful not to disturb the primitive campsite so Hurst wouldn't know someone was onto him. This was as close as Mozart had ever been to catching him. He considered calling Cookie and seeing if he'd come up and help him, but decided against it. Cookie and Fiona were still working through Fiona's issues, and he didn't want to disturb them when they had a rare week off.

Mozart eased himself into the chair on the front porch of the small office building. He'd noticed that each night the people staying in the cabins generally gathered around the office to chat. He wasn't one to crave the attention of others, but he wasn't ready to go back into his cabin yet. The evening was beautiful.

Mozart held a beer loosely in his hand and watched as a SUV pulled into the parking lot. Three women climbed out. They were the kind of beautiful that came from hours spent at the spa and in the bathroom before stepping a foot outside. They were all wearing skin-tight dresses and high heels. They looked like they'd just spent a night out celebrating something. The cabins weren't exactly the Hilton, so Mozart wondered briefly what had brought them there. Being a man, he also admired the way their dresses showed off their bodies. It'd been a while since he'd been with a woman, and these were some fine looking specimens.

"Oh shit, Cindy," the woman in the blue dress said a bit too loud, "he looked hot from the car, but you can have him, I wouldn't be able to look at him while fucking him." All three of the women giggled drunkenly.

"But you could always have him do you doggy style then you wouldn't have to look at his face," the woman, who was apparently Cindy, said. "I'd do him, look at his muscles!"

Unfortunately, Mozart had gotten used to those kinds of harsh comments from women since he'd been injured. He chugged the rest of his beer and shifted to stand up and leave. He didn't care what they thought, but he wasn't going to sit there and listen to it. The shallow comments from the women didn't deserve a response.

Before he could move, he felt a hand slide over his chest from behind in a tender caress and felt a woman lean over him.

Before Mozart could say or do anything, he heard a husky voice say from right behind his right ear, loudly enough for the three bitches to hear, "Come on, honey, those three orgasms you gave me before dinner weren't enough. I can't believe you can stay hard that long. Before you call for the jet can we have one more round in the shower?" The mystery woman nuzzled the side of his face, his scarred side, as she playfully ran both hands up and down his chest.

Mozart's body locked tight. His teeth clenched and he could feel his jaw clench. Even not knowing exactly what the woman's game was, her tone, and words, made his cock stand up and take notice. He brought up a hand up and wrapped it around one of her forearms as she continued to caress him with her other hand. Mozart didn't know if he wanted to wrench it away from his body, or force it down lower into his lap. He did neither, just held on as her hand moved up and down his chest and he watched as the bitches' mouths dropped open and they stared as they walked past him on their way into the small office.

The woman who had her hands all over him apparently wasn't quite done. As the trio passed by, he felt her head turn toward them as she sneered in their direction, proving she knew they could hear her the entire time, "He's *all* man, and he's *all* mine. If you're stupid enough to not be able to look past his face, then you don't deserve to have a man spend all night pleasuring you. And *believe* me, he knows how to use every *inch* of his body for *my* satisfaction."

The woman then stood up, grabbed Mozart's hand, and pulled him off the porch toward his small cabin. Mozart didn't even look back to see what the other women did, he only had eyes for the dynamo who was towing him to his room.

Summer's heart was beating at what felt like a million miles an hour. What this man must think of her. But she couldn't stand there and let those bitches say those things about him. While Summer didn't really know him, she felt as if she has a small connection to him. After all, she'd been cleaning his room and handling his linens…linens that had been up against his body. No one deserved to be treated that way.

Summer had no idea what happened to him and how he'd gotten the scars on his face, but she had a feeling he was probably military of some sort. He had that look about him and maybe he had some sort of PTSD and that's why he went on the long walks in the woods. Those women being rude to him felt wrong on so many levels. He was always polite to the employees at the motel. He was neat. He was quiet. But if Summer had stopped to actually think about what she was about to do, she never would've done it. She was pretty embarrassed, but she had to keep going until the women were gone.

When they reached the door to his cabin, Summer stopped, took a deep breath, and turned around to face the big man who was still holding her hand.

Mozart watched as the woman in front of him took a deep breath before she turned around. He grinned. Now that he could see her face, he knew exactly who she was. She was the maid for the cabins. He waited for her to speak.

Summer tugged at her hand, but the man wouldn't let it go. She looked up at him a bit nervously and watched a crooked smile take over his face, and all the words in her brain fizzled away.

"Do you think I could know the name of the woman to whom I gave three orgasms and apparently pleasured all night long?

Summer nearly choked. God, she was embarrassed. "I'm so sorry about that back there," she quickly said. "Those women were such bitches; I just wanted them to be jealous as hell and to realize what they were missing. I didn't mean to embarrass you or anything. I really am sorry." She trailed off when she saw he was still smiling.

"Your name?" Mozart demanded in a low voice.

"What?"

"What is your name?" he repeated easily, seemingly not upset in the least.

"Summer," she told him without thinking. Shit, maybe she shouldn't be blurting things out without thinking first. It had always gotten her into embarrassing situations in the past, seemed like she hadn't learned her lesson after all these years.

"Summer," Mozart told her, "I'm not embarrassed. I think that was one of the nicest things anyone has done for me in a long time. Don't be sorry. Shit, don't be sorry. I'll never forget the looks on their faces when you said jet. I just wish I had it all on film to show my buddies."

Summer chuckled a little, still feeling embarrassed and very aware he still held her hand. It felt awkward, but at the same time it didn't. "I don't know what came over me. I'm not usually like that. Anyway, well, I'll be going…" she trailed off and attempted to once more remove her hand from his, but he still wasn't letting go. She looked up at the man questioningly again.

"Come to dinner with me." It wasn't exactly a question; it came out more like a statement.

"What?" Summer couldn't have heard him right. She knew she sounded silly asking him to repeat everything, but she was confused.

"Come to dinner with me, Summer," the man said again.

"But you don't even know me," Summer said in bewilderment.

Mozart laughed a little. "But Summer, I gave you three orgasms before dinner."

Summer blushed and looked down. "Jesus, I'm never going to live that down am I?"

Seeing Summer's embarrassment, Mozart got serious. He put his finger under her chin and lifted it so she was looking at him, noticing she didn't fight him. "You're too easy to tease, but please, let me take you to dinner to thank you. You didn't have to step in there for me. It honestly doesn't bother me what people say about me, but you didn't know that. You went out on a limb for me. Please let me treat you to dinner in return."

Summer looked at the man again. He was serious,

she could tell. She *was* hungry. It didn't matter where they went, she hadn't had a good meal in forever. She tried one more time to dissuade him.

"But I don't even know your name."

He finally let go of her hand, only to immediately hold it out to her again. "I'm Mozart, nice to meet you, Summer."

"Mozart? Can you play piano?"

Mozart laughed and continued to stand there with his hand out. He'd stand there all night if he had to. He'd forgotten how fun it was to pursue a woman. He hadn't had to do it very often and it made him feel ten feet tall. If Summer knew how cute she looked and how her actions only made him more determined, he knew she'd be mortified. "Go out to dinner with me and I'll tell you how I got my nickname."

Summer smiled and shook her head in exasperation. He was crazy, but she was finding she liked his brand of crazy. Finally, she put her hand in his and shook it. "I think that's blackmail, but you have a deal."

Apparently, they were going to dinner.

MOZART ENDED UP taking Summer to a local steak place. It wasn't fancy, but the food was good. He'd already been there a few times and had enjoyed everything he'd eaten. Maybe even more important, the restaurant was quiet and Mozart felt like he could get to know Summer a bit better. The hostess had sat them at a booth in the back and asked what they wanted to drink when they'd arrived.

"Get whatever you want," Mozart told her when he saw her hesitate.

"I guess I'll just take a water." At Mozart's raised eyebrows, Summer hurried to defend her selection. "It's fine. I'm hungry and don't want to fill up on soda or alcohol."

Mozart nodded and ordered a beer. After the waitress had left to collect their drinks, he turned back toward Summer and just watched her as she read over the menu.

"You aren't going to even look at the menu?" she asked Mozart nervously.

"Nah, I've been here a couple of times and know what I want."

The way he said he knew what he wanted made Summer nervous for some reason, but she didn't call him on it. Maybe it was how he looked into her eyes as he'd said it instead of looking at the menu itself. Summer looked down at the menu as if it held the answer to world peace and tried to ignore Mozart's presence and steely gaze.

When the waitress came back with their drinks, Mozart ordered an appetizer of cactus dip with chips and a

Rib Eye steak with potatoes and spinach. Summer asked for a sirloin, medium rare, with a baked potato and fire-roasted green beans.

After the waitress left, Mozart leaned his elbows on the table and asked, "So, how long have you worked at the motel?" As a get-to-know-you question, it was pretty tame, but Summer was embarrassed anyway. She'd grown very adept at handing out vague answers that sounded like she answered the question, but never really gave much away.

"I've been there for a while now. It's okay, but not something I want to do the rest of my life. You've been there a while, what are you doing up here in Big Bear?"

"Oh you know, just enjoying some time off and hiking in the woods."

Summer nodded, she'd figured that was what he was doing there. Something didn't ring true about his answer, but it wasn't as if she could call him on it when she was trying to avoid answering any deep questions about herself either.

"Have you seen any animals when you've been out there?"

"Yeah, quite a few deer, but no bears."

Summer laughed. "I guess that's good then."

Mozart just nodded and watched the woman across from him. She never stayed still. She fiddled with her water glass, then put her napkin in her lap. Mozart could see her leg moving up and down with nervous energy. On the outside, Summer seemed composed and calm, but he could tell she was nervous just being with him. He liked it. Not that she was nervous, but that she *cared* enough to be nervous.

"Tell me something about yourself, Summer."

"Oh, um…" she shrugged, "there's not much to tell really."

"Bullshit. Come on, give me something here." Mozart really wanted to know this woman. Not the superficial crap, but something about her he wouldn't find out unless he pushed.

"My middle name is James." At his look of incredulity, Summer put her head in her hand in embarrassment.

"James?" When she didn't immediately explain, Mozart leaned across the table and smoothed a piece of hair behind her ear. "Summer James. I like it."

Summer raised her head and looked at the gorgeous man across from her. She honestly had no idea what had possessed her to come to his defense back at the motel. He was obviously a man who could take care of himself. He didn't need her jumping in trying to make those women jealous. Mozart was easily the buffest man she'd ever seen. He probably could've flattened them with only a look. But she just *had* to be a hero. She sighed, knowing since she'd blurted out her embarrassing middle name she'd have to explain.

"My parents wanted a boy. They convinced themselves I *was* a boy. They didn't want the doctor to tell them the gender of their baby, convinced they already knew because of old wives tales or something. So they had my name all picked out already. James. It was a disappointment when they found out I was actually a girl. They didn't have time to really think of a good name, so they chose Summer since it was July when I was born. They kept James because they'd become so attached to it."

"Summer is a good name."

Summer whipped her eyes up to Mozart's and looked at him in confusion. That wasn't what she expected him to say.

Mozart expounded on his statement. "You said they didn't have time to think of a good name. I disagree. Summer is a great name. It fits you. Your hair is blonde, you have the bluest eyes I've ever seen, the blue of a beautiful summer day. Your skin is tan...I don't think I've ever met a woman whose name fits her better than Summer fits you."

Oh. My. God. Summer thought she was going to melt into a puddle right there in the booth. Mozart was looking at her in that intense way he had again. Summer felt goose bumps break down her arms. She hadn't been fishing for compliments, but he'd given her a doozy of one. "Uh, thanks," was all she could squeak out. Summer was saved from having to say anything else because the waiter arrived with their food.

Summer ate as slowly as she could, but her steak was so good. It'd been forever since she'd eaten such a good meal. It was if she could actually feel her body soaking in the nutrients from the meal as she ate.

Mozart watched Summer eat. It was obvious she was enjoying the food, but as he paid more attention, she enjoyed it a little too much. They weren't talking a whole lot, which was fine, but Mozart could tell Summer was purposely trying to slow herself down, to not eat too fast. She'd take a bite to eat, then put her fork down against her plate, and rest her hands in her lap as she chewed. It was methodical and purposeful. Mozart pressed his lips together in consternation. He'd been there a time or two in his life. Almost the entire team had been captured during a mission and they'd been half starved. For almost a month after they'd been rescued he'd had to force himself not to gorge himself every time he'd sat down to eat.

His body had told him to eat as fast as he could, but his mind fought and tried to tell him there was plenty of food and he didn't have to hoard it or scarf it down. Mozart hated seeing that same dilemma in Summer's actions. He knew he wouldn't say anything about it though, it would embarrass her, and the last thing he wanted was for her to be embarrassed.

"So, what's your last name Summer James?" Mozart wanted to soak up every scrap of information he could about this fascinating woman.

"Pack."

"Summer James Pack. I like it."

Summer merely shrugged. It wasn't as if he had to approve of her name, although she supposed she was glad he didn't hate it. "So, you told me you'd tell me the story about your nickname if I came to dinner with you."

Mozart put his fork down and pushed his plate back. He leaned toward Summer and put his arms on the table. He was pleased to note she continued to eat as he started his explanation. "I'm a Navy SEAL," he began, satisfied when she merely nodded instead of fawning all over him as many women did after hearing what he did for a living. "It's commonplace for men in the military to be given a nickname. Typically the names are tongue-in-cheek jokes or modifications of a person's name, or even an out-and-out reminder of some dumb-ass thing the person did."

"Which category does Mozart fit into?" Summer asked with a smile on her face.

Laughing Mozart said, "Unfortunately, the last one." He continued with his story, loving the smile that crept across Summer's face. "One night, after we'd made it through Boot Camp, me and a bunch of the other seamen went out and got completely hammered. We'd been working our butts off for a few weeks and we were all young kids. We ended up at a karaoke bar." Mozart paused, enjoying the hell out of the wide smile on Summer's face. When she smiled a real smile, it lit up her whole face.

"Yeah, we thought we were all that and a bag of chips, and apparently I refused to leave the stage after singing three songs. The patrons were noticeably pissed and one guy yelled, 'Hey Mozart, get off the stage and let someone else slaughter a song for a while.' That was it. That's all it took. The name stuck. So my one foray into the land of music ended up marking me for life."

"I'm sure there's a karaoke bar somewhere in Big Bear. We could always find it after dinner."

"Oh, hell no, Sunshine. I'm pretty sure if you heard me sing, your ears would bleed."

Summer put her fork down and sighed. She could probably eat more, but she knew she'd regret it if she stuffed anything else down. Mozart was funny. She'd never have guessed he had such a good sense of humor when she'd first seen him. It just reminded her that everyone had more depth than could be seen on the surface. "So what's your real name?"

"I'll tell you only if you swear you won't use it."

Summer looked taken aback. "What? Why?"

Mozart smiled to take the sting out of his words. He was serious, but he didn't want her to feel as if he was mad or anything. "I have five friends on my SEAL team. We all have nicknames. Three of them have women. For the most part, the girls refuse to use our nicknames. Wolf, Abe, and Cookie don't care, but it's been so long since I've been called anything other than Mozart, it makes me feel as if their women are talking to someone else when they insist on calling me by my given name."

Summer decided to tease him. She didn't really care what she called him, but wanted to give him crap. "What is it? Fred? Winston? Oh no, I have it. Sherman?"

Mozart reached across the table and grabbed her hand and playfully pretended to bend her index finger back in retribution. Summer giggled and tried to pry her hand out of Mozart's grip with no luck.

"No, smartass. It's Sam. Sam Reed."

"Sam." Summer loved the feel of her hand wrapped up in his. He made her feel…safe. "It's so normal."

Mozart let go of her hand reluctantly and sat back and crossed his arms across his chest.

"Normal?"

"Yeah. You don't look like a 'Sam' to me. You look like you'd have some bad ass name."

"Like what?" Mozart was enjoying the hell out of the conversation.

"Um...maybe Jameson...or Chase or Blake." Getting into it, Summer continued, "I know, what about Tucker or Trace?"

"Jesus, Summer. Seriously? I look like a *Jameson*?" Mozart said through his laughter.

"Okay, maybe not, but I'm not sure I can call you Sam either, it's just so...plain."

"Well then, it's a good thing you *don't* have to call me Sam. You promised."

"Actually, I didn't. You assumed." When Mozart opened his mouth to rebut her, Summer reassured him. "Kidding! I'll call you Mozart. No worries."

"Thanks, Sunshine, I appreciate it."

Summer smiled at the big man sitting across from her. Sunshine. Her ex had never called her by any nicknames. He'd always just called her Summer. She didn't realize how much she liked hearing a pet name until Mozart had said it to her...twice.

"Come on, you about ready to go?" Mozart asked, putting his used napkin on the table.

"Yeah, thank you so much for dinner. I appreciate it, even though it wasn't necessary."

"Of course it was. You stood up for me. It doesn't happen much. Usually people go out of their way to steer around me. You waded right in and put yourself between me and those women. Although, it must be said, you shouldn't make a habit of it. You have no idea what someone will do. They could've turned against you, or I could've been a dick about it and dragged you in my room to make you put your money where your mouth was."

"I can read people pretty well; I didn't think that would happen."

"Want to take the leftover rolls back?" Mozart changed the subject, knowing she believed every word she said about him and that she'd probably do the same thing over again. He didn't think she'd ask to take the extra food home, but somehow he knew she both needed and wanted them.

"Sure, if you don't mind." Summer tried to shrug nonchalantly, knowing the bread would be her lunch, and probably dinner, the next day.

When the waiter put the check on the table, Summer made an effort to reach for it so she could pay for her own dinner, not that she really had the money, but she felt like she should at least let Mozart know she wasn't expecting him to pay for her food.

"Seriously?" Mozart asked with a raised eyebrow, reaching out and snagging the bill before Summer could open the folder to look at it.

Summer just looked at Mozart and said, "Yeah, You don't know me, there's no reason for you to pay for my meal."

Mozart pulled out his credit card and put it in the

folder and laid it on the end of the table. "I asked you to dinner, I'll pay. Believe me, I appreciate you even offering. I can't remember a time when a woman even made the suggestion, but it still irritates me that you'd think for a second I'd *let* you pay."

Summer just looked at Mozart for a second, then, not knowing what else to say, she whispered, "Thank you."

"You're welcome. You should always expect a man to pay when he takes you out, Sunshine."

"That's not the way of the world today, Mozart."

"Well, it's the way of *my* world."

Summer could believe it. Mozart was intense in a "take charge, Alpha man" kind of way. She wanted to hate it, but couldn't. She'd never had anyone treat her that way before and it was almost scary how much she enjoyed it. Summer didn't say anything when the waiter returned with the credit card slip and Mozart signed it. He stood up and held out his hand for her as she scooted out of the booth.

Summer took hold of Mozart's hand and he didn't let it go as he walked them out of the restaurant and back to his truck. He waited until she stepped up and into the passenger seat and got settled before closing her door and walking around to the driver's side.

They drove back to the motel in a comfortable silence.

They pulled up in front of his cabin back at the hotel. Mozart watched as Summer got out of the car and self-consciously smoothed her hair over her right ear.

"Thanks for the dinner, Mozart, I appreciate it."

"You're welcome. How are you getting home?"

"Oh, I stay here on the premises."

"You do?" Mozart looked around in confusion. He couldn't see where she might be staying, unless she was living in one of the cabins or if there was a room in the office area, which he hadn't seen when he'd been in there eating breakfast.

"Yeah. Thanks again for tonight…have a good rest of your vacation. Be careful out there hiking. Don't piss off any bears, okay?" Summer smiled nervously up at Mozart, hoping he'd let the matter of where she lived drop.

"I will, Sunshine. Thank *you* for sticking up for me with those bitches tonight."

"I see now you didn't need me to do anything, but seriously, I hope you don't see yourself as flawed in any way. Believe me, you are *not* flawed."

"Are you flirting with me, Summer?" Mozart teased, thrilled at the blush that crossed her face.

"Uh, no, I…"

"I'm teasing you, Sunshine. I don't really think about it anymore and it honestly doesn't bother me when people look at me weirdly because of it. With that

43

being said, anytime you want to throw down with bitches who look at me the wrong way, I won't object."

Summer just shook her head at him and smiled. "Have a good night, Mozart."

"You too, Sunshine." Mozart watched as Summer walked toward the office and disappeared around the side of the building. Was she related to the owner? Where exactly was her home? What made someone as pretty and intelligent as Summer seemed to be, work at a run-down motel such as this one? Mozart had a ton of questions, and not enough answers.

Mozart went into his cabin. He had enough on his plate at the moment, too much to really even have the time to think about Summer's mysteries, but he couldn't help it. She'd gone out on a limb tonight for him. He'd been honest with her when he'd told her that he couldn't remember the last time someone did something like that for him without wanting anything in return, other than his teammates of course.

He lay back on his bed and thought back over the night. There were little things bothering him about Summer. She didn't wear a coat, even though it was a bit chilly. She wasn't wearing any makeup, not that was a big deal, but most women he knew would at least make an attempt to put something on. Summer's clothes seemed a bit big on her, like they were the wrong size. She tried not to show it, but she was hungry tonight.

Mozart also hadn't seen her around at night before, so how had she just popped up tonight? And while he hadn't really *seen* her before tonight, her actions had now put her in his crosshairs. There was something about her. Something that made him want to be the man that would give her three orgasms and would pleasure her all night long. Mozart knew it was crazy. He wasn't the type of man to pursue women; at least he wasn't before his accident. He hadn't had to. They always came to him. But he was curious about *this* woman, and wanted to solve the mystery. He *would* solve it before he left.

If Summer knew what Mozart was thinking, she probably would've found a way to leave that night. But she figured it was the last time she'd see him. He was most likely leaving soon and that would be that. Summer was forgettable. She knew it. It'd been proven to her time and time again in her life. He'd be no different. She *knew* it.

She snuggled down into the sleeping bag she'd bought at the thrift store. It smelled slightly musty, as if it'd been sitting in the store for a while, but it was warm, and at the moment that was all that mattered to her. She fell asleep thinking about Mozart and ended up dreaming about him as well.

Chapter Four

THE NEXT DAY Mozart was up early, as was his usual, and he was on the trail before the sun rose. If he wanted to catch Hurst, he knew he had to sneak up on him unaware. The man was lethal and Mozart couldn't underestimate him.

As he hiked silently, Mozart thought more about Summer. He was heading back to Riverton tomorrow. His leave was up, and as much as he hated to leave his search for Hurst, he was equally loathe to leave before really getting to know Summer. It was crazy, he'd lived the past nineteen years wanting revenge for Avery and nothing had ever stood in the way of that. But one encounter with Summer was all it took for his interest to be piqued and for his intense drive for revenge to slip a bit.

She was an enigma. She was well spoken and smart, yet she was working at a run-down motel as a maid. Mozart shook his head. He didn't understand, but he would. He wanted to talk to her before he left. He wanted to reassure her he'd be back. Mozart knew he'd be coming back to continue trailing Hurst, but if he was honest with himself, he knew it was also because of Summer.

Mozart wanted to introduce Summer to his friends, and *that* was unusual for him. He kept the line straight and narrow between his real life and his sex life. The women he slept with knew the score, they knew their encounter was one night. Sometimes he kept one around for longer than that, but he told them upfront that he wasn't relationship material and if they wanted to stick around and sleep with him for a while, he wouldn't be opposed, but he always told them they'd never get more than that out of him.

Surprisingly, as much of an asshole it made him sound, most women were okay with the arrangement.

Mozart shook his head and brought himself back to his present surroundings. He had a feeling his days of sleeping around were gone, all because of a too-thin mysterious woman who had no idea how beautiful she was. He'd track her down when he got back to the motel and let her know his plans. His plans to come back and get to know her better.

MOZART STEPPED OUT of his truck into the dirt parking area at the motel. He sighed and ran his hand through his hair. He'd found Hurst's campsite for a second time, but the man had cleared out before Mozart could get there. Mozart had been so close, but once again, he was too late. He'd already called Tex and updated him on what he'd found. Tex had reassured him he was on his trail and they'd get him, but Mozart just shook his head and didn't agree or disagree.

He'd heard it time after time and he was no closer today than the cops were all those years ago. Mozart wondered for the first time in his life if the bastard would ever be caught. He thought again about his teammates and their women. Could he one day be as happy as they were? Would finding the woman meant to be his, somehow make up for not avenging Avery? Mozart had no idea, and he wouldn't figure it out today, but it was something to think about. For the first time, he allowed himself to admit that he was tired. Mozart's life was passing him by, but he didn't really know how to stop it.

Mozart looked around at the cabins to see if he could find Summer. He saw her cleaning cart parked at the last cabin. He started toward where he hoped she was. Mozart hadn't seen anyone else cleaning the rooms since he'd been there, so hopefully the cart meant Summer was inside the room.

He wished he didn't smell so…funky…but he'd been hiking all day and couldn't help it. Since he'd checked out that morning, he wouldn't have a chance to shower before he headed back down to Riverton.

Mozart peered into the cabin and smiled at what he saw. Summer was making the bed and swearing at it under her breath.

"Stupid sheets. Why do the beds have to be so damn heavy? Jesus, most normal people wouldn't demand their entire sheet set be cleaned every day, but *this* guy? Of *course* he did. Dammit!"

"Need some help?" Mozart said laughing.

Summer spun around with a screech, and seeing Mozart, scolded him with a hand on her chest, "God, you scared me! Don't *do* that!"

Mozart smiled. When was the last time any woman had spoken to him in that tone of voice? He couldn't say. Most women, and men for that matter, were scared of him. The women would always simper and do whatever they thought he wanted them to do while men typically just went out of their way to avoid him.

"Sorry, Sunshine. Didn't mean to frighten you," Mozart told Summer softly, still leaning nonchalantly against the doorjamb. "I just wanted to let you know I checked out today and will be gone for a while."

When Summer simply looked at him he continued, "I didn't want leave without letting you know."

Mozart was nonplused when she responded with, "I knew you checked out when I went to clean your room and saw everything gone. Why would you come back to tell me?"

Summer was honestly confused. Usually when people checked out, she never saw them again. Every now and then someone would come back because they left something in their room and they'd seek her out to see if she'd found it, but never had someone come back to tell her they were leaving. "You left your keycard in the room, you don't have to turn those in. It's not a big deal." When Mozart didn't respond, Summer continued hesitantly, "Is that why you came back? To give me your keycard?"

Mozart took a step into the room and came toward Summer. He noticed she took a small step back, but then caught herself and stood her ground.

"I came back because I like you. Because I wanted to see you again. Because I think I want to be the one who gives you three orgasms before dinner for real. That's why." Without waiting for Summer's response, Mozart took two steps until he was right up against her and reached a hand out to tag her behind her neck. He pulled her close so their lips were almost touching.

"I couldn't leave without tasting you at least once." Mozart's lips were over Summer's before she could say anything. Summer was mid-gasp so it made it easy for him to slide his tongue over her lips and into her mouth.

Summer groaned, her situation and where they were fell away instantly. She couldn't think about anything other than how good Mozart felt. Her arms came up hesitantly and flattened on his chest before she ran them up and clasped them together behind his neck.

Mozart was about to pull back when he felt Summer's tongue come out and shyly slide over his. There was no way he could stop now. He groaned and pulled her closer to him. Mozart tightened his hand around her neck and pressed his other hand into the small of her back, forcing her into his body until they were touching from head to hips. He deepened the kiss and felt Summer shift against him restlessly.

Mozart felt satisfaction curl through him. Summer apparently wanted him as much as he wanted her. He couldn't hide his erection from her, but her squirming told him she was just as turned on as he was. Running his tongue over hers one more time, Mozart slowly pulled back, not letting go of her waist or neck, but separating their mouths.

"I'll be back, Summer. I want you. I want to see where this can lead us, and for once in my life, I'm not talking about a one-night stand."

Summer slowly opened her eyes and looked up at the man whose arms she was engulfed in. She took one hand from behind his neck and put it on his scarred face. She rubbed her thumb over the worst of the scars.

She was flattered beyond reason, no, she was thrilled this gorgeous, virile man wanted *her*.

"Okay," she whispered with a shy smile.

Mozart finally removed his hand from her back and took her face in both of his and rested his forehead against hers. "Stay safe until I can get back to you."

Summer just nodded.

Mozart leaned down and took her lips in one last hard kiss before letting her go and backing up. They kept eye contact with each other until he reached the door of the room and disappeared into the parking lot.

Summer sat down hard on the un-made bed. "Holy Hell," she said softly aloud to the empty room, "that man is lethal!"

Chapter Five

SUMMER WAITED. MOZART said he'd be back. The weather got colder and he didn't return. She didn't know what happened, but she wasn't completely surprised. A part of her wanted to believe Mozart. He'd seemed so sincere, but Summer should've known. All her life people seemed sincere when they'd told her things like, "I'll call you," or, "we'll go out for lunch," but more times than not, they didn't call and they didn't ask her out for lunch. So Summer wasn't entirely surprised, but found herself depressed about Mozart's absence all the same.

She knew it was time to move on anyway. The weather up on the mountain was cold, even for southern California. Many people assumed since it was in California that it'd be warm all year, but in actuality, this area had some of the best skiing in the state in the winter months. Starting in November, Henry had cut her salary in half, which was ridiculous because it wasn't as if she was making that much to begin with, but

Summer was pretty much stuck until the spring because she had no transportation and the cold weather made it that much harder to up and leave. Nevertheless, she'd already decided she'd be going.

But for now, today, Summer felt like crap. She knew she was sick, who wouldn't be after living in the kind of situation she was? She wasn't eating enough, and the storage building was freaking freezing. Summer had stuffed paper towels into the cracks trying to keep the cold air out, but it wasn't doing much good. Henry had given her an old space heater and let her run an extension cord from the office into the storage building, but she didn't use it a lot. It didn't seem safe. However, there were times at night when she was just so damn cold that she had no choice.

Summer didn't have any friends in the small town because she was kept busy cleaning the cabins, and even when she wasn't working, it wasn't as if she had transportation to get anywhere to meet people. She was stuck, and it was definitely time to go. As soon as it got warmer and she could save up enough money for a bus ticket, she was getting out of there. What had seemed like such a great idea a few months ago, now just seemed stupid. Summer was an intelligent woman, and if she knew of anyone else in her situation she'd just shake her head at them and call them an idiot.

She lay on her cot and snuggled down deeper into

her sleeping bag. She closed her eyes and re-lived the kiss Mozart had given her the day he'd left for the thousandth time. She'd never been so attracted to anyone before in her life. Even her ex-husband had never made her feel like that in all the years they'd been married.

Summer had made good money and they'd been equals in their relationship, almost *too* equal. Summer sighed, remembering how she'd felt when Mozart had hauled her into him and not given her a choice about whether or not she wanted him to kiss her. She wasn't an idiot, she'd read plenty of romance books where the woman was submissive to the man...and she'd scoffed at each one. But now, remembering how she'd felt in Mozart's big arms, she was rethinking her beliefs. Just remembering him telling her to "be safe" as he left her standing in the cabin, was enough to make her insides quiver. No one had ever cared if she was safe before, and it felt good. Too bad he hadn't meant it.

Summer fell asleep once again thinking about the man who'd turned her nice plain life upside down, and then left without looking back.

MOZART SAT AT the table at *Aces Bar and Grill* with his friends and sighed. He wasn't really in the mood to hang with his teammates, but he'd promised he'd be here, so here he was. Caroline and Wolf had come back from their honeymoon looking relaxed and happy. Fiona and Cookie had also settled into married life. Fiona seemed a lot more relaxed while out in public, so obviously her sessions with the therapist had done her a world of good.

Mozart thoughts turned back to Caroline. He re-membered how she'd trusted him to sew up her wound when she'd been injured on the plane that had been taken over by terrorists. Mozart hadn't ever experienced that sort of trust again...until Summer. It wasn't as if he'd had to sew up a knife wound or anything, but she'd taken his hand and let him bring her to dinner. She'd let him kiss the hell out of her, and she'd melted in his arms. Summer wasn't scared of him, and had stood up for him when she hadn't even known who he was.

Mozart gritted his teeth. Fucking hell. He'd told Summer he'd return to Big Bear to see her, and he hadn't been back. He argued with himself over it daily, but he hadn't had the time. No, that was a lie, he hadn't *made* the time. Yes, he and the team had been sent on a few missions since he'd been up to the lake, but that honestly wasn't an excuse. It wasn't that far to drive and Mozart could've honestly made it up there in a few hours on his downtime.

He'd convinced himself that whatever connection they had was all in his head. Mozart had only taken one woman home since he'd met Summer, and it was a complete disaster. All he could think of was Summer and how she'd lit into those women for him. Recently, when he'd caught the woman he'd been about to bring to his bed looking at the scars on his face in disgust, Mozart lost his erection and any desire to get naked with the woman immediately. He'd told her to get out and he'd lain on his bed thinking about what a mess his sex life had become since meeting Summer.

"What the hell has you thinking so hard over here, Mozart?" Benny asked, sitting down next to him with two beers. He handed one to Mozart and took a drink out of the one still in his hand, waiting for his friend to answer.

"You wouldn't believe me if I told you, Benny."

"Try me."

"I met a woman…"

Benny burst into laughter, interrupting Mozart's explanation. "When don't you meet women?" When Mozart didn't say anything Benny looked at him incredulously. "Shit, seriously? You too? I'm gonna be the last one of us left the way you all are falling so hard."

"I didn't say I was gonna marry her, jackass," Mozart mumbled throwing back the beer and almost finishing it off in one gulp.

"Yeah, but you're *you*, Mozart. You're the flirt. You're the one who takes care of the ladies when we're on missions. If you've got one woman on your mind above all the others, you're screwed. You've already tagged and branded her in your mind. You just have to catch up and do something about it."

Mozart put the mostly-empty beer bottle on the table and stared at Benny thoughtfully. Was he right?

"Let me put it this way," Benny continued, unconcerned about the turmoil going on in his friend's head. "When did you see her last?"

"About two months ago."

"And when was the last time you got laid?"

Mozart didn't answer, thinking back. Jesus. Yeah, he'd taken that one woman home, but he hadn't been able to follow through. It'd been about two and a half months since he'd actually had sex.

"About two months, right?" Benny pushed.

"You are one scary guy, Benny," Mozart commented, pushing his chair back and crossing his arms over his chest.

"Look, just because I have this ridiculous nickname doesn't mean I don't see stuff. Mozart, you're my friend. As much as I make fun of the other guys for being tied down to their women, I think it's great. I'd give anything to be where they are. I see how content and happy they are and I can't help but want that for myself. Stop fighting yourself. If you've found someone who makes you reconsider pulling your dick out for any woman that wants it, I say you need to explore that."

"That was certainly a crude way of putting it, but I get it." Mozart felt the pit in his stomach swell to an almost unbearable size. He lowered his voice and fingered his scarred cheek. "I told her I'd be back, and I haven't been. I hurt her. I know I did."

"Then make it right, Mozart." Benny stated matter-of-factly. "Look at Alabama and Abe. She forgave him for the asshole thing he did to her. If this woman is meant to be yours, she'll forgive you too, but you have to go to her. If you don't give her a chance, you'll never know."

"Jesus, Benny, I feel like you're Doctor Phil or something."

Benny just laughed and slapped Mozart on the back. "Yeah, well, I don't want to hear all the mushy details, just go and talk to her. See if she's feeling half of what you are. If she is, you can see about making it work. If not, you're no worse off than you are now. But at least you can move on if you know."

Mozart nodded. "I'll see if the Commander will give me the weekend. I'll head up to Big Bear and talk to her."

"Big Bear? Isn't that where you went up to look for Hurst?" All of the team knew about Hurst and Mozart's mission to make him pay for what he'd allegedly done to his sister. Mozart had told them where he'd been during their week off when they'd all gotten back. There were no secrets from the team. "Do you think he's still up there?"

"Yeah, I found evidence of a campsite, but he'd left by the time I had to get back here. Tex has been working on leads and says he's not sure he's left the area, but he doesn't have a lock on him yet. He could be a thousand miles away, or he could be wintering up there at the lake."

Benny's face turned serious as he put his beer on the table next to Mozart's empty one. "If you need us up there to help track him, all you have to do is ask."

"I know, and I appreciate it. I think this time I'll just head up here to see if Summer is still there. I wouldn't blame her if she ditched that crappy motel and left for warmer weather."

"All I'm saying is if you need it, we have your back."

"I appreciate it, Benny, seriously."

They nodded at each other and Mozart stood up to head over to Wolf and Ice to let them know he was headed out. He congratulated both of them once again, and when Caroline stood up to hug him goodbye, Mozart bent her over his arm just to irritate Wolf. Laughing when Wolf snatched Caroline back into his arms as soon as Mozart stood her up, Mozart told them he was on his way out.

"I talked to the Commander and he's thinking we'll

be headed out next week," Wolf warned.

"Got it, I'm only going up for the weekend; I'm not tracking…this time. I'll keep you up to date and I should be back on Monday."

"Is everything all right?" Caroline asked with worry in her voice.

Mozart picked up her hand and kissed the back of it. "Everything's fine, Ice. And just because I know you're nosy, I'm going up to see a woman."

Caroline rolled her eyes. "I'm sorry I asked. You aren't satisfied with all the bitches throwing themselves at you down here? You have to drive into the mountains now?"

Mozart simply smiled. He loved how Caroline wasn't afraid to speak her mind around him or the other SEALs. "What fun would that be?" He wasn't about to tell her the real reason he was headed up to Big Bear.

Ice rolled her eyes, as he expected. Mozart gave a chin lift to Wolf and said his goodbyes to the rest of the team and Alabama and Fiona. As he headed out the door, he wondered what kind of reception he'd get from Summer. Lord knew he didn't deserve for her to be glad to see him, Mozart just hoped she would be anyway.

Chapter Six

I T WAS LATE Friday night by the time Mozart arrived at the cabins up in Big Bear. He pulled into the familiar parking lot and noticed only a couple of cabins had lights on in them. The office also had a light shining dimly through the grimy window.

Mozart pulled his jacket around him and zipped it up as he stepped out of his truck. It was cold, the wind was blowing, making it seem at least twenty degrees colder than it actually was. There was no snow on the ground, but it was probably only a matter of time. Once the snow fell, the cabins would most likely become a bit busier because of ski season, but generally people who came up to this area to ski would choose a more well-known and popular hotel to stay at, rather than the run down, locally-owned motel.

Mozart strode up to the office door and tried the door. It opened and a bell tinkled above his head as he entered. The space was empty, but it wasn't too long before someone came out of a room in the back of the small building. Mozart recognized the man as the owner of the motel. He'd chatted with him briefly the last time he'd been up here.

"Hey, I remember you. Need a room?"

Mozart refrained from rolling his eyes at the desperate sounding man. Of course he remembered him. He was big and mean looking and had a huge scar on his face. Mozart wasn't the kind of man that anyone would forget. "Maybe. I'm looking for Summer. She was the maid the last time I was here. Does she still work here?"

Henry looked upset. "Why? What did she do? Did she take something?"

"Jesus, no. Why would you automatically think that?" Mozart was pissed. He didn't really know Summer, but he didn't think there was a chance in hell she was a thief, and he was mad that it was the first thing this guy thought of. After what had happened to Alabama he was hyper-sensitive about people being accused of stealing with no provocation.

"Sorry, man, I just didn't know why else you'd want to know if she was still here."

"*Is* she still here?" Mozart growled with barely concealed impatience, wanting to reach across the scarred counter and shake the man.

"Yeah, she's still here. You want me to get her?" Henry placated, as if he knew Mozart was on the edge of losing his temper.

"No. Just tell me where she is."

Without even thinking that it might not be a good idea to tell a large pissed off stranger where a woman was living, Henry jabbed a thumb toward the building next door. "She stays in the storage building."

Mozart took a step back as if the man had hit him. "What? What building?"

"You know, the little storage building. She gets to stay there as a part of her salary. Free of charge. You know, room and board without the board."

"Are you kidding?"

"Uh…no?"

Mozart just shook his head and turned on his heel toward the door.

"Will you need a room tonight?" Henry called out behind Mozart.

Mozart stopped. He wanted to give this man money like he wanted a hole in the head, but he also wanted to be near Summer. If Summer was staying on the property, he wanted to as well. He spun back to the short man standing behind the counter. "Yeah, one night. If I'm going to stay another, I'll let you know."

Henry turned to the ancient computer and punched a bunch of buttons. "Credit card?"

Mozart pulled some twenties out of his wallet and threw them down on the counter. "Cash."

"Oh, okay. Uh, I'll put you in number seven, there's

no one on either side of you, so it should be quiet." When Mozart didn't say anything Henry looked down and hurriedly swiped the keycard to program it. He held out the paper for Mozart to sign, and sighed in relief as he pocketed the key card and turned to head out of the office. "Breakfast is from seven to nine, winter hours," Henry called as the door shut behind the large man.

Mozart clenched his teeth together and looked to his right as he exited the small office. He took a hard look at the small storage building set back from the office a bit. He'd never really looked at it before, because he had no reason to. Why would he? It was a fucking storage building, not a place where anyone should be living. Mozart didn't like what he saw.

He took in the ramshackle building at a glance. It was probably about a hundred square feet, at most, and had one door with no windows. There was an old fashioned lock on the door. As he walked up to the building, Mozart couldn't believe anyone was actually *living* inside it. The owner had to be wrong.

There were no electricity lines leading into the roof of the shack, but looking closer, Mozart could see an orange extension cord snaking from the office into a crack in the back of the building.

Mozart held on to his temper by the skin of his teeth. There was no damn way this was safe, or even legal. He hoped like hell he wasn't going to find Summer in this hovel, but he was afraid he was going to be disappointed.

SUMMER SHIVERED INSIDE her sleeping bag. She couldn't get warm. The wind felt like it was whipping through her little building as if she had the door open. She'd given up on the space heater because it had started making such horrible rattling noises she was afraid if she fell asleep with it on, it would burn down the building she was sleeping in.

Her head spun. She'd been dizzy for a while, but tonight it seemed worse. She wasn't sure what was wrong with her, but there wasn't any way to find out either. Henry expected the cabins to be cleaned, and it wasn't as if she could call in sick. She had no money or transportation to get to a doctor anyway.

Summer nearly jumped out of her skin when she heard a brisk knock at the door. No one ever knocked on the door. The guests just assumed it was a simple storage building, and if Henry needed her, he typically just yelled out the back door of the office for her.

"Who is it?" Summer asked tremulously.

"Mozart. Open the door, Summer."

"Oh. My. God," Summer whispered. Shit could he really be here? *Why* was he here? She couldn't see him now. Raising her voice so he'd hear her she asked,

"Why, what are you doing here? Do you need something?"

"Yes, I need something, Sunshine. Open the fucking door." Mozart tried not to lose patience with Summer. He could hear the surprise and yes, even a little fear in her voice.

"I don't think…"

"Don't think. Just open the door." Pausing a beat, he tried to tone down his impatience and pleaded with her. "Please? I want to talk to you. I *need* to talk to you."

"Can't it wait until morning?"

"No."

"I'll be right there, we can talk outside." Summer sat up on the cot and unzipped the sleeping bag. Shit, it was freezing. There was no way she was letting Mozart in her little space to talk. She'd go and meet him outside and maybe they could go into the office, or into his truck, or somewhere else to talk. She didn't care where it was, as long as it was warm.

Summer swung her legs out of the warm haven she'd been cocooned in and leaned over to the flashlight sitting on the corner of the sink. She clicked it on and the beam shone upward, illuminating the small space. Summer stood up and stuffed her feet into her sneakers. She still had her clothes and socks on, so she was as ready for this late night visit as she'd ever be. She shuffled over to the door and fumbled with the latch.

Summer opened the door and went to step out, but was pushed back by a large body stepping into her space.

Mozart knew Summer wouldn't want him inside. He had no idea how he knew that, but he did. That made him all the more determined to *get* inside. As soon as the door opened a crack, he was there, pulling the door open gently and stepping into Summer's space.

"Step back, Sunshine. I'm coming in."

"Oh, um…" Summer didn't have a chance to say anything else before Mozart was there, inside the little building, making it seem twice as small as it actually was. She watched as his eyes roamed around, taking everything in at a glance, before settling in on her. She shivered, as much at the look in his eyes as with the cold.

Seeing Summer shiver shook Mozart out of his stupor. He immediately unbuttoned his jacket and eased it off his body. He took hold of Summer's shoulders and turned her so her back was to him. "Arm," he told her gruffly. When she held an arm up, he steered it into one sleeve and did the same to the other as she lifted that one too. He wrapped the coat around her and pulled her back into his arms.

She felt even skinnier than when he'd held her in his arms a few short months ago. Summer was shivering lightly and Mozart could feel her swaying where she stood. Mozart wrapped his arms around her a bit more tightly, holding her snugly against him, willing his body heat to sink into her skin.

"I'm sorry, Sunshine." It wasn't what he'd planned to say. Mozart had an entire speech planned about how busy he'd been, how many missions he'd been on and how he'd wanted to come back and see her, but couldn't. But seeing how she was living and the condition she was in, only made him want to kick his own ass. The apology was for so many things, the least of which was for not coming back up the mountain as he'd said he would.

Summer, being Summer, didn't ask why, didn't make him grovel, but simply nodded and said, "Okay."

Mozart turned her around to face him and put one hand on her shoulder and tipped her chin up with the other. "I'm really sorry, Sunshine. I said I'd be back and I wasn't before tonight."

Summer merely shrugged, "It's okay, Mozart. I didn't think you meant it."

Mozart's hands tightened on her. "What do you mean you didn't think I meant it? I said it didn't I?"

"People say stuff all the time. I've found most of the time they don't follow through."

"Well, when *I* say something I follow through. I should've been here before now though. I let you down."

"Mozart…"

Knowing she was going to let him off the hook again, he interrupted her. "No. Tell me you believe me. Tell me you know that when I say something, I do it."

At the stubborn look in her eyes, and her lips pressing together Mozart could only laugh. "Okay, that sounded conceited I know, but I hate having you think that nobody does what they say they will." Mozart wrapped her up in his arms again and picked her up as he sat down gingerly on the rickety cot. He put Summer in his lap and kept his arms locked around her. Without saying anything else he took a second look around the small room.

The space heater sat forlornly in the corner, silent and turned off. The orange extension cord was plugged into it as it snaked under the edge of the boards that made up the wall. There was a sink, but it was old and cracked. There were shelves lining the back and sidewall over the sink, filled with bottles of cleaning materials and cloths of some sort. There was a suitcase sitting against the back wall as well. It was closed, but not zipped.

Mozart closed his eyes and leaned his head against the side of Summer's. She'd lain her head against his chest and sat on his lap awkwardly with her hands in between them, clutching his jacket around her.

Standing up suddenly with Summer in his arms, he gripped her tightly as she startled. "Shhh, I've got you,

Sunshine. Do you need anything for the night?"

"Uh…no?"

At her answer, Mozart took a step to the door and leaned over so Summer could reach it. "Open the door for me, please." Summer did as he asked and Mozart walked out into the cold night with Summer held tight against his chest. He shut the door behind him with a kick of his boot and took long strides toward cabin seven. He dropped Summer's feet to the ground when he got to the door, but didn't let go of her waist. Keeping her body close to his, Mozart took the keycard out of his pocket and slid it into the slot on the door. It clicked and Mozart pushed it open.

Summer didn't say a word as Mozart carried her across the parking lot and opened one of the cabin doors. He put his hand on the small of her back and guided her into the room once he'd opened the door. He kept walking until he got to the small bathroom.

"Take a hot shower, Sunshine. I'll get you something to wear when you're done. Get warm. I'll be back. I'm going to make a short trip into town. Don't open the door to anyone. I mean it. If your boss knocks, ignore him. Take your time in the shower. Got it?"

Summer could only nod at Mozart. She was bemused and a bit in shock. She hadn't expected to see Mozart again, but here he was. She knew he wasn't really *asking* her to do anything, he was telling her. At the moment, she had no issues with his demands though. She felt like crap and was cold down to her bones. A hot shower sounded heavenly.

She watched as Mozart leaned down and brushed his lips over her forehead. "In you go. I'll be right back with something for you to wear. I'll put it right outside the door here. Then I'm going into town."

"Okay, Mozart. Thank you." Summer knew she should be protesting his Alpha tendencies, but she couldn't.

"Don't thank me, Sunshine. This is all on me."

"What is?" Summer was confused. "What are you talking about?"

"Go on, get in the shower. We'll talk when I get back."

"God, you're annoying," Summer huffed, finally showing some backbone, as she tried to pull out of his arms to do as he'd demanded.

Mozart laughed and whispered, "I'm sure I'll annoy you more as we get to know each other, but just remember I always have your best interests in mind."

"Whatever," was all Summer could come up with as a comeback. It was lame, but the shower was calling her name and she really was freezing.

Mozart let go of Summer and watched as she walked into the little bathroom and shut the door behind her. He blew out a breath and put both hands up into his hair and raked his hands over his head. Jesus, all this time she'd been living in a hovel and he'd been making excuses as to why he shouldn't come back up here. Mozart should've thought more about her situation that night when he'd taken her to dinner. All the signs had been there, but he'd ignored them. Some observant Navy SEAL he was. God, he was a fucking idiot.

He was here now and he'd fix this. Mozart would make sure she wasn't hungry or cold again. He wasn't sure she was going to like his solution, but he didn't give a damn. She was *his*, dammit. She was vulnerable, yet spicy at the same time. She wasn't a young naïve woman in her early twenties, she was like him. Seasoned. The combination was intriguing to Mozart. He hadn't thought twice about her being his. She just was. As soon as he'd seen her trying to act as if nothing was out of the ordinary with her living in a shack and telling him she had no expectation for his return, he'd known.

Mozart walked out to his truck and grabbed his bag along with a bottle of soda he'd forgotten to drink on his way up to the lake. He re-entered the cabin and remembered to crank up the heat in the room before he did anything else. The overly warm room might make him uncomfortable, but he'd bet Summer would appreciate the added warmth. Mozart smiled at hearing the shower running. He could imagine Summer stand-ing under the spray of water naked as the day she was born. He willed his erection to go down as he pulled a T-shirt out of his bag. Usually he didn't wear any underwear so he didn't have a pair of boxers she could wear, not that they'd have fit her anyway.

He dug some more and came up with a pair of shorts that he usually ran in. He knew they'd be huge on her, but he also didn't want her to feel vulnerable without something covering her lower half. Mozart went over to the bathroom door and eased it open. Steam rolled out the door and he couldn't help but smile again. He knew he'd told Summer he'd leave the clothes outside the door, but he couldn't resist going into the bathroom if his life depended on it.

"Sunshine? I'm leaving a shirt and stuff on the sink. I brought in a soda as well. Drink it. The sugar will do you good." When she didn't immediately answer, he called out, "You okay?"

He heard a muffled shriek and watched as she stuck her head around the shower curtain. She obviously hadn't heard him when he'd opened the door to talk to her.

"Mozart? Get out of here!"

"Okay, I'm going. I just wanted to make sure you were all right before I headed out. There's clothes on the sink, and drink the soda I left for you."

"All right. Just go!"

Summer heard Mozart laugh as he shut the bathroom door. She should've been more upset at him, but she couldn't be. She hadn't been able to take a lazy shower in what seemed like forever, and it felt heavenly. Summer grabbed the cheap little shampoo she'd left in the room earlier that day, and washed her hair twice, using the bubbles from the lather to scrub her skin as best she could. She conditioned her hair and rinsed that out as well.

Then, cranking the knob so the water was even hotter, Summer sat down and let the stream beat on her back as she huddled in the bottom of the tub. She moaned as the water hit her shoulder blades and massaged her muscles.

Not knowing how much time had passed, Summer finally reached behind her and turned off the water, but sat still for a moment or two. The bathroom was completely filled with steam, she could barely see an inch in front of her face. She'd been cold for so long the heat felt heavenly. Finally, she stood up, wobbling from both the heat and hunger, and peered out the shower curtain, making sure she was alone.

Seeing the door was still shut, she pulled back the curtain and reached for one of the towels. It was small and scratchy, but Summer didn't care. Once she was dry, she pulled Mozart's T-shirt over her head and laughed as it fell mid-thigh on her. She tried putting the shorts on, but knew immediately there would be no way they'd work. They were miles too big and she had no way to keep them up. She left them sitting on the counter and prayed Mozart was as much of a gentleman as he'd been so far. Summer didn't want to be completely naked under the shirt, so she pulled her panties back on.

Seeing the soft drink sitting on the counter, her mouth immediately started watering. She wasn't much of a soda drinker, but at that moment, she thought she'd die if she didn't drink it right that second. She twisted the top off, enjoying the hiss of the carbonation as it rushed out of the bottle. Summer tipped it up and guzzled the fizzy drink down. It was slightly warm, but it tasted so good. She finished the bottle and sighed happily. Her sigh was immediately followed by a gigantic burp. She blushed, hoping like hell Mozart wasn't sitting out in the room laughing.

Summer cracked open the bathroom door, watching how the steam rushed out of the bathroom as she pushed it all the way open, and walked into the small motel room. Mozart wasn't back from wherever he'd gone yet, so, avoiding the bed, she wandered over to the easy chair in the corner and pulled her knees up to her chest as she stretched the huge T-shirt over her knees so she was covered from neck to toes.

She knew Mozart had questions and wasn't happy with how he'd found her. Summer hadn't done anything wrong, but knew he'd want to talk to her about it. She just had to figure out how much she was going to tell him. Summer didn't usually blurt out her entire sad life history to just anyone. She wanted to trust Mozart, but she also remembered how much he'd hurt her by promising to be back, and then not showing up until now.

Summer cocked her head to the side as she thought about Mozart. He *had* come back. He'd never said how long it'd be before he returned; only that he would. So technically, he hadn't broken any promises to her. Summer sighed. She'd play it by ear and see what he wanted when he got back. Maybe Mozart just wanted her to be warm for the night. He was a SEAL after all; it was ingrained in him to rescue people. Maybe he wasn't back for anything, other than to fulfill his promise or to go hiking some more.

She hated waiting. Mozart would return soon enough. Lying her head against the side of the chair, she quickly drifted off to sleep, secure in the knowledge that, for the moment at least, she was safe and warm.

Chapter Seven

MOZART JUGGLED THE bags in his hands as he opened the door to his motel room. He'd driven into town to find some food. He knew Summer would never admit it, but she had to be hungry. He hadn't seen any food in the damn storage building she'd been living in, and of course, he remembered how she'd enjoyed the steak when they'd gone out two months ago.

The room was dark, except for the light coming from the open bathroom door. Mozart looked around and found Summer curled up in the chair in the corner of the room. He silently put the bags of food down and went over to where she slept. Mozart kneeled down in front of the chair and put one hand on her knee, still covered by his shirt, and the other on the arm of the chair. He rubbed her knee softly, trying to bring her out of sleep slowly so she wouldn't be scared.

"Summer? Wake up, Sunshine." Mozart grinned as she grunted in her sleep, and turned her face deeper into the side of the chair. "Come on, wake up."

Summer squinted at Mozart, then closed her eyes again. "Do I have to?" she sighed, sounding much whinier than she wanted to.

Mozart grinned. God, she was cute. "No, not really, but I did go and find a twenty four hour grocery store, and I brought back food."

Summer's eyes popped open comically. "Food? What kind of food?"

Mozart ran his hand down the side of her cheek. He wanted to find her actions funny, but he couldn't. Most women he knew would've been perfectly happy to fall back asleep, but he knew first-hand when your body was craving calories, food always came before sleep.

"Sit up and see for yourself, Sunshine."

Summer shifted upward and straightened her knees. The shirt rose up and off her knees, but luckily still covered her adequately. Mozart hadn't moved from her side and his hand was now resting on her bare knee. They stared at each other for a moment.

"Your scar looks better," she said quietly as she brought her hand up and fingered the worst of the scars on his face.

Mozart grunted. "Yeah, Ice insisted on me rubbing some crappy cream on it every night. I keep telling her it doesn't matter, but she won't give it up. I do it just to shut her up."

"Well, it seems like she knows what she's talking about. It really does look better, Mozart." Suddenly thinking he might think it mattered to her, Summer quickly backpedaled. "Not that it looked bad…"

"Shhhh, it's fine." Mozart put his fingers across her lips stopping her from saying anything else that might make her feel she was digging herself into a hole. "I know what you meant. I give Ice crap, but the cream does actually make it feel better." At the look of relief on Summer's face Mozart continued, "Now, come on, get up and see what I got for us. I didn't stop on my way up here, so I got a bit of everything." Summer would never know he was lying about not stopping to eat, but he didn't want her to feel bad about all the stuff he'd bought.

Summer stood up and would have fallen over if Mozart hadn't been there to steady her. "Whoa, take your time. I'm sure the heat of the shower made you woozy. Let me help."

Summer was too embarrassed to say anything else, and if she was honest with herself, she was just too damn hungry to care too much. She let Mozart lead her over to the bed.

"Here, sit, while I go through the bags."

Summer sat and watched Mozart bend over and grab the bags with one hand. He sat sideways next to her on the bed with one knee bent and the other foot propping himself up on the floor. He reached into the bags and pulled out a loaf of bread, a small jar of peanut butter, a six pack of V8 juice, a jar of dill pickles, two cans of corn, green beans, and carrots, two boxes of granola bars, a package of provolone cheese, sliced turkey, a salad in a bag, a small bottle of ranch dressing, and a bag of green apples and oranges.

Mozart looked up sheepishly at all the food scattered around them on the bed. Summer threw back her head and laughed. "Jesus, Mozart, I thought you just went out to get a snack?"

Summer wasn't ready for Mozart to lean over and put his hands next to her hips. He kept coming forward until Summer had no choice but to lean back and put her weight on her hands behind her, or let him run right into her. Mozart had a serious look on his face. She thought he'd laugh with her about the food, but apparently she'd read him wrong.

"You aren't eating enough. You're even thinner than you were when I held you in my arms a couple of months ago. I don't like it. I bought what I thought would last without being refrigerated. Except for the salad and the cheese and turkey, everything will keep in that damn hut you're living in. You need more protein. I don't like that you get dizzy when you stand up, and I certainly don't like that your only bed is a broken cot with a sleeping bag in a building that has holes in it.

And I *really* don't like the fact that your only source of heat is a scary looking heater that's this far from burning down the entire structure." Mozart held his thumb and index finger about an inch apart in order to punctuate his last thought, then leaned forward again. "I don't know why I care so much, but I do. I can't explain it any more than I think you can, Sunshine. I made a mistake in not coming for you sooner, but I'm here now, and you can bet I *see* you now. I don't mean to freak you out, but I'm not going anywhere."

Summer could only watch with wide eyes. She *should've* been freaking out at his words. She was an independent woman who could take care of herself, but she wasn't doing a very good job of it lately, and she was tired. She wanted nothing more than to let this man take care of her. If that meant she was weak, so be it. Summer was hungry, tired, and cold. At the moment, Mozart was offering to lighten all three of those burdens. She'd take what she could get and hope for the best. Summer said the only thing she could at the moment. The only thing she was thinking. "Okay."

"Okay?" Mozart looked confused.

"Okay."

A smile slowly came over Mozart's face and he shook his head as he leaned back, allowing her some space. "You're gonna keep me on my toes aren't you, Sunshine?" He didn't give her time to answer. "Now, what do you want to eat?"

Summer sat up looked down at all the food sur-rounding them. "The salad." She'd eaten so much crap over the last few months and her body was craving the vegetables. "And a can of green beans. Then an orange for dessert."

"You got it. Sit still, I'll get it ready for you." Mozart moved off the bed, but not before running his large hand over her head and pushing a strand of her blonde hair behind her ear. He then turned his attention to the food and used some tool he'd pulled from his belt to open the can of green beans. He handed it to Summer with a plastic fork, before opening the bag of lettuce. Mozart watched out of the corner of his eye as Summer dug into the can. Once again, he saw how she tried to control herself and not inhale the food, but she had a little less control tonight than she'd had when they'd gone out to eat.

Mozart dumped the lettuce in a big plastic bowl he'd also picked up at the store and opened the cheese and turkey as well. He tore off pieces of the meat and cheese and included it in with the lettuce. He stirred in more dressing than she'd probably normally use, but she needed the calories.

Mozart handed her the doctored lettuce and another plastic fork and sat down on the bed next to her, peeling an orange as she ate. They didn't say anything, just enjoyed each other's company in silence. Mozart couldn't help but feel a little cavemanish. He'd gone out and gotten food for his woman. He was providing her with food, warmth, and a safe place to sleep, everything psychologists said was vital for a person's wellbeing.

Summer put aside the bowl of salad she'd practically inhaled and sighed. She was full, but she still craved the sweetness of the orange, its smell now permeating the air around them. She reached for the fruit only to have Mozart hold it out of her reach.

"Open," he demanded in a low harsh voice.

Summer looked up only to see a look of determination and desire on his face. "I can do it, Mozart."

"I know you can, but I want to. Now open."

Summer looked in Mozart's eyes and saw he wasn't going to budge on this. She opened her mouth and moaned as she bit into the first slice of the orange Mozart put into her mouth. She opened her eyes and blushed. Mozart's erection couldn't have been more obvious, but he wasn't hiding it from her in any way. His legs were spread, and he was sitting sideways on the bed again.

Seeing where Summer's eyes had strayed, Mozart smiled at her. "I can't help it, Sunshine. The noises that come out of your mouth are sexy as hell. But I'm a patient man. I'll wait as long as it takes you to be comfortable with me. But be forewarned, that doesn't mean I won't be pushing you and trying to make you comfortable with me sooner rather than later."

He held out another piece of orange to her. Instead of answering his conceited remarks, Summer leaned forward and grabbed Mozart's wrist. She held on to it without breaking eye contact with him and took the piece of orange into her mouth. She shifted it to the side and suckled his finger into her mouth at the same time. She licked around his knuckle and nipped at the tip before drawing backward and letting go of his wrist. "I'm not sure why you think it's going to take a while for me to be comfortable with you, Mozart. I feel more at ease with you than I did with my ex, who I'd been married to for ten years."

Summer watched fascinated as a muscle ticked in Mozart's jaw. One hand was clenched in a fist so tight his knuckles were white. She watched as he brought the finger she'd just had in her mouth up to his lips and sucked it into his own mouth. Without breaking eye contact with her he unclenched his other fist and brought it up to the back of her neck, drawing her closer to him. Summer loved when Mozart did that, granted he'd only done it once before, but she hadn't forgotten the feeling. It was controlling as hell, but it comforted her, without a doubt.

"Are you finished eating, Sunshine?"

Summer nodded in the confines of his pseudo-embrace.

"Here's what's going to happen. I'm going to put the food away and you're going to climb under the covers. I'll get changed and come back to you. We aren't going to make love tonight, but you'll sleep in my arms. We'll get to know each other better and when we both know it's right, I'm going to take you so hard you won't remember anyone else and you'll certainly never think of having anyone else. Got it?"

Summer shivered in delight and answered him in a whisper, "Got it."

"Jesus, Sunshine. I gotta know before I let you go. You wearing anything under my shirt?"

Summer giggled and shook her head. "The shorts were too big, but yeah, I put my undies back on."

"God. Okay, I'm getting up now, scoot yourself up and climb in. I get the right side; it's closer to the door."

Summer did as Mozart directed, not taking her eyes off him the entire time. She watched as he gathered up the food and put it on the dresser. He went into the bathroom and she heard the toilet flush and him brushing his teeth. Finally, Mozart cut the light off and the room went dark. She felt Mozart climb into the bed beside her. Summer hadn't thought about his statement about taking the side of the bed closer to the door when he'd made it, but now, lying in the dark, knowing he was between her and anyone that might try to get in, made goose bumps break out all over her body. No one had ever done that sort of thing before. Her ex wasn't into protecting her in any way, figuring she could do it herself.

Summer lay stiff in the bed, wondering what Mozart's next move was going to be, but she didn't have to wait very long. He rolled over and gathered her into his arms. He didn't turn her so her back was to him, he just pulled her right into his embrace.

Her arms were between them and she could feel he'd taken his shirt off. Summer flattened her hands on his chest and snuggled her head into the indentation between his neck and shoulder. She sucked in a breath, loving how he smelled. "You're so warm."

Summer felt him nod and kiss her head before putting his head back on the pillow. "Shhhh, go to sleep, Sunshine."

"I have to get up by eight so I can get some breakfast," Summer sleepily murmured.

"I said, shush. Don't worry about tomorrow. I'll take care of it."

"Okay...Mozart?"

He sighed a disgruntled sigh. "You aren't sleeping."

"I just wanted to say...thank you for coming back. People usually don't."

Mozart held Summer closer to him and couldn't find the right words to say, so he stayed silent until

Summer fell asleep in his arms. Only then did he whisper into the silent room, "I'm sorry it took me so long. I'll always come for you, Sunshine."

Chapter Eight

SUMMER WOKE UP the next morning slowly. The room was lit up with the light of the sun. She immediately knew it was way later than it should've been. She was going to miss breakfast if she didn't hurry. If she missed the food that Henry put out for the guests, she knew she wouldn't get a chance to eat. She rolled over, remembering suddenly that she wasn't in the little storage room.

Summer felt better than she had in a long time. Her belly wasn't trying to eat itself and she was warm. Not only that, but for the first time in months, her back didn't hurt. The mattresses in the cabins might not be top-of-the-line, but they were damn sure better than the cot she usually slept on. Summer snuggled deeper into the covers, not even caring, for once, that she was probably going to miss breakfast.

Mozart wasn't in the room. Summer remembered waking up a few times in the night and rolling over, only to have him crowd her and wrap his arms around her again. She thought she even remembered him whispering soothing words to her, but she couldn't remember anything he might have said. She rolled over and smelled the pillow where his head had been resting. God, she had it bad.

Summer sat up and scooted so her butt rested up next to the headboard and looked around. The bags of food were sitting on the small dresser against the wall. The TV was old, but still worked just fine. She could see Mozart's bag on the floor next to the dresser, the sight of it comforting her, because it meant he hadn't left.

She was surprised to see her own suitcase sitting next to his duffle though. Mozart had obviously gone out to the storage building and retrieved it for her. At least she could put on some of her own clothes now. As much as Summer wanted to continue to wear Mozart's T-shirt, she knew she'd have to put her own clothes on sooner rather than later.

She threw back the covers, for once not shivering in the cold morning air, and padded to the bathroom. It was amazing how nice it was not to have to go outside and into a different building just to pee.

Summer had just exited the bathroom to go and grab her stuff out of her suitcase so she could get ready, when the door opened. She froze in place, then sighed in relief when she saw it was Mozart.

"Hey," she said and then took a step back as Mozart

came toward her. He had a serious look on his face and he didn't stop until she'd backed up into the wall.

He came up against her and put his forearms on the wall on either side of her head. This brought his mouth so close to hers, if either of them moved an inch, they'd be touching. "Good morning, Sunshine. Sleep well?"

Summer could only swallow hard and nod silently.

"Good. You like this room?"

Not knowing where he was going with his questions, she answered, "Uh, yeah, it's fine."

Mozart smiled and took one arm off the wall and brushed her hair back from her face and smoothed it behind her ear. "Good. You'll be staying here for the winter."

She tipped her head to the side. "What?"

"You heard me, you're staying in here instead of that damn shack."

"No, I'm not," Summer argued, getting pissed.

"Yeah, you are. I had a little talk with Henry this morning, we came to an agreement."

"That's just it. *You* came to an agreement. I didn't. I can't afford to stay here." Summer didn't like that Mozart was in her space now. At first she'd loved how protective he seemed to be, but she was seeing the drawbacks of that now.

"I know you think I'm being controlling, but listen to me for a second. Please?"

Jesus, if Mozart had demanded and yelled she could've resisted him. But pleading with her to listen? Shit. "Go on."

Summer watched as Mozart suppressed a smile, but before she could blast him for it, he continued. "I talked with Henry about the unsanitary conditions you've been living in. I don't think he was surprised by anything I told him, but I did get his attention when I said I'd already talked to the Better Business Bureau."

Summer gasped. "You didn't!"

"Of course I didn't, but *he* didn't know that. All I told him was that because all the rooms weren't being rented out every night in the winter, it was the least he could do to allow you to stay in one of them. You'll be responsible for cleaning it, of course, and he still isn't budging on the meal thing, but at least you'll have a warm and safe place to sleep." Mozart stopped. He'd wanted to wring the old man's neck. He hadn't given a shit that Summer was freezing to death and practically starving. If Mozart had his way, he'd take Summer back down to Riverton tonight, but he knew in his gut she wouldn't agree. She was prickly and independent.

"I can sleep here?"

The incredulous way she'd asked made Mozart's blood boil. No one should ever think that living in a crappy motel like this one was an answer to their prayers. "Yeah, Sunshine. You can sleep here. And you can put your stuff here. You'll be living here until the spring, or until you find something else." He had to tack that that part on, because he hoped against all hope she'd want to find something else…down the mountain in Riverton.

"I don't know what to say."

Mozart leaned in close to her again. "Say, 'Thank you, Mozart,' then kiss me to thank me properly."

Summer grinned. "Thank you, Mozart." She leaned toward him and at the last minute shifted until her lips met his scarred cheek.

Mozart laughed and grabbed her around the waist and took two steps backward and fell on the bed on his back, still clutching Summer in his arms. She shrieked and laughed as they fell. He bounced once and clasped her hips to his.

Summer sat up and gazed down at the man beneath her. She could feel Mozart's muscles tense under her. He'd manhandled her as if she were a child, and a part of her loved it. She could tell he'd moved so he didn't hurt her, but he was definitely in control. Even now as he was holding her to him. She couldn't move if he didn't let her, but she wasn't worried. Summer knew if she made the slightest move or in any way gave him an indication she didn't want to be right where she was, he'd let her go.

The T-shirt she was wearing had ridden up her

thighs as she straddled him. She was still decent, barely. Mozart's hands spanned her waist and his thumbs were rubbing back and forth on her stomach. She shifted and felt him grow hard under her. The only thing keeping them separate were his jeans, whatever he was wearing under them and the small piece of cotton covering her womanly parts.

"I promised myself I'd take things slow with you, Sunshine, but you're making it hard."

"I can tell." Summer grinned and shifted in his lap again, feeling how "hard" she was making it.

Mozart's head went back and thunked on the bed. "I knew you'd be a wildcat in bed. I didn't mean to bring us here yet, but I'm not sorry we're here." He lifted his head back up and looked at her. "You have no idea how difficult it was for me to leave you in bed this morning. You were lying next to me, curled into my arms. One leg thrown over mine and I could feel your heat against my leg, just as I can now. If I hadn't promised both of us that we'd take it slow, I'd be buried so deeply inside you, you wouldn't know where you ended and I began."

"Mozart," Summer whispered, more turned on than she'd ever been in her life. She ran her hands over his chest, rubbing against him as he continued to speak.

"I'm not proud of my history, Summer. You'll hear about it sooner or later, and I'd rather you heard it from me. I've slept with way more than my share of women, but none of them meant anything. I've never thought twice about sleeping with them and leaving in the morning. I've never looked back. Not once. Until you. I'm sure when you meet my friends they'll delight in letting you know what a man-whore I've been, and they won't be lying. But I swear to you, right here, right now, that's all behind me. I haven't been with anyone since I met you two months ago. Since losing my virginity, I've never gone for two months without sex. I know how that makes me sound, but please believe me. You've crawled inside me and won't leave. I don't want you to leave."

"I..."

"No, let me finish." Mozart moved one hand from her waist up to the back of her neck. It seemed to be his favorite place to grab hold of her. "I want to have sex with you more than I want anything in my life. But, it's not happening this weekend. I have to leave on Sunday. I have to go back to work. I want to prove to you, and to myself, that I'm a different man. That you've made me a different man. I want to be with you because of who you are, not to use you for sexual release. Don't get me wrong, I want that too, but I want to get to know you more."

Mozart brought Summer's head down close to his face using his grip on the back of her neck. She braced herself on his chest. "I want you, Summer. I want all of you. I want you in my bed. I want you in my house. I want you to get to know my friends until they're your friends too. I want to wake up to you hogging the covers every morning. No matter what it takes to get there, I'm willing to do it. If I thought you'd do it, I'd haul your ass down to Riverton before you knew what was going on. But I think I know you enough to know you don't want that. What I'm not willing to do is rush this, to make you think I'm here for a quick fuck and that's it. I'm not willing to leave you up here in some damn run-down fire-trap of a shack knowing you're shivering and hungry every night. I need you to let me help you. Please, God, let me do this so I can sleep at night knowing you're all right up here."

Summer melted against Mozart's chest. Breaking eye contact, she rested her forehead against his chest and took a deep breath. Mozart didn't move his hand from her neck and his other hand was now sweeping up and down her spine in a soothing motion.

"Thank you, Mozart," Summer said, repeating her thanks from earlier. "I don't doubt you're popular with the ladies. I have no idea what you see in me and why I'm any different from any of them." When she felt him take a breath as if to answer her unasked question, she brought her head up and put one finger over his lips to shush him. "Will you do me a favor?" At Mozart's immediate nod, Summer continued, "I'm willing to try this, whatever this is, but if at any time you find someone else who you want to hook up with, please let me go. I won't be able to stand it if you change your mind and don't tell me. I'm a big girl. Just tell me and I'll leave you alone."

"I'm not going to change my mind, but if for some reason we aren't working out, I'll tell you." They looked at each other for a long moment. "But this is exclusive. You're mine for as long as this lasts, Sunshine. It goes both ways."

Summer could only nod. She felt as if she were in an alternate world. A world where she was a femme fatale and men threw themselves at her feet begging her to choose them. It was ridiculous; no one had ever been passionate about her, until now. "If I'm yours, then you're mine too."

"Damn straight," Mozart answered. "Now, thank me properly, woman." Loving the smile that crept across Summer's face at his words, he brought her lips to his. Mozart devoured her. He kissed her as he'd never kissed a woman before. In the past, he'd only tolerated kissing as a stepping stone to getting to the good stuff. Now, with Summer, kissing *was* the good stuff. He tasted her, loving it when her tongue came out to play with his. He nipped and licked and ultimately controlled the kiss. He was playful one moment, and forceful and demanding the next. Finally, he pulled back a fraction. "Jesus, Sunshine, I could eat you alive. You're my match in every way."

He felt Summer smile and he turned them over until she was under him. Seeing her hair spread out on the mussed covers turned Mozart on even more. He was so hard, he literally hurt. He couldn't remember ever being this turned on, and it'd happened with just a kiss. Mozart felt Summer's hands running over and squeezing his ass. He clenched his teeth and warned, "Watch it, Sunshine, you're playing with fire."

"I haven't been burned yet," she cheekily shot back.

Mozart took one hand and shoved it under her, and taking a risk, under her panties as well. Her skin was warm and smooth as he smoothed his thumb over her cheek. Mozart wanted to do so much more, wanted to delve his hand lower between her thighs and see for himself if she was as turned on as he was, but he behaved himself...barely. "We need to get out of this room before I do something I swore I wouldn't."

Summer just smiled up at him. "I have to work, Mozart," she reminded him gently.

Mozart didn't frown or act disappointed in any way. "I know, Sunshine. I'll help you get the rooms clean, then we can play." When she froze under him Mozart cocked his head and queried, "What?"

"You're going to help me? I thought you might go

and do…something. Hike, something, while I worked."

Mozart shook his head. "Nope, I came up here for you. You're stuck with me until Sunday night."

"Seriously?"

Not understanding why she was so surprised, Mozart answered gruffly, "Yes, Summer. Is it so hard to believe that I'd want to help you clean the rooms?"

"Actually, yeah. It's just…I thought you came up here to do…whatever…and you were glad to see me while you were here."

Mozart clenched her ass harder and shoved her into his erection. "No, I'm here for you. No other reason. There'll come a time when you won't doubt my feelings for you. I see you and get hard. I smell you and get hard. Hell, I *think* about you and get hard. No, I'm here for *you,* Sunshine. And the sooner we stop talking about it and get our butts out of bed and clean the damn rooms, we can get to know each other better and I can get you back in bed and not let you up for air until we're both so exhausted we don't know our own names."

Giggling, Summer told him, "That was a long, run-on sentence, Mozart."

Mozart rolled his eyes and murmured, "That's what I get for having the hots for a smart woman." Then louder, he told her as he slowly got to his feet, "Get up. Shower. We have time to run and grab some breakfast at this kick ass little hole-in-the-wall café I found before we have to start cleaning."

He pulled Summer to her feet and playfully shoved her toward the bathroom. "Go on, I'll wait outside for you. If I stay in here while you're naked in the shower, I'll definitely break my promise." Mozart kissed Summer once more hard, then headed for the door. As he opened it, he looked back and said, "You've got fifteen minutes, Sunshine. Better hurry." He winked at her once more before shutting the door behind him softly.

Summer collapsed against the wall. She had no idea what Mozart saw in her or why he'd decided he wanted her, but she'd ride the ride for as long as she could. She'd be crazy not to. Shaking her head, she hurried to her suitcase on the floor and pulled out a pair of jeans, a long sleeved henley and undies, and headed back to the bathroom. Summer had no doubt that if she took longer than Mozart's allotted fifteen minutes he'd be back in the room just as he'd warned.

She smiled. Keeping him on his toes would be fun.

Chapter Nine

SUMMER SAT BACK in the booth and sighed. She'd just stuffed herself with the best omelet she'd ever eaten. Cheese, green peppers, bacon, fajita chicken, onions, tomatoes, and sausage, all smothered in more cheese, sour cream, and salsa. Mozart had ordered the special, which came with two eggs, bacon, sausage, and a small stack of pancakes.

"I don't think I can move."

"You can move. We've got rooms to clean, then shopping."

"Shopping? For what?"

Mozart looked at Summer, knowing what he was going to say would piss her off, so he kept it as vague as he could. "Stuff you need."

Summer crossed her arms over her chest, not buying his vague response. "Stuff I need? What kind of stuff?"

"Give me your hand." Mozart put his hand on the table palm up.

"What?"

"Give me your hand, Sunshine."

Without thinking, Summer took one hand and reached across the table toward Mozart. When his voice got low like that and he ordered her around, something inside made her cave every time.

Mozart grabbed her hand tightly and put his other over hers. He learned forward as he spoke. "Stuff you need. A microwave. A hot plate, food. A warm jacket. Stuff. You. Need." When Summer tried to pull her hand out of his, Mozart tightened his hold. "I know you don't want to accept it. I know you feel bad and are embarrassed. But that's not going to stop me. If I'm going to leave you up here, I have to know you're eating. That you're warm. That you're okay."

"Mozart, you got me a room to stay in. I'll be fine."

"You should've had that fucking room all along. I can't go home, can't go on my missions knowing you're not eating. I can't believe you lived in that fire-trap of a storage shed for as long as you did."

Summer took a deep breath. Mozart was right. She was embarrassed as he'd said. She tried one more time. "Mozart, Henry hired a new handy-man, he's working on making the building safer. He's helped me out a lot. I'll be fine."

"I don't see *him* living in a run-down shack with no bathroom or electricity. Where's this handyman living? Where's Henry living?"

"Well, I don't know."

Without giving Summer a chance to say anything else, Mozart said, "Exactly. They're not living in that piece of shit. They're eating three meals a day. They have warm clothes. They're not you."

They stared at each other for a long moment.

"I don't like not being able to get those things for myself." Summer finally said quietly.

Mozart sighed in relief. "Jesus, you think I don't know that, Sunshine? You have 'independent woman' written all over you. But you don't get that I want to do this for you. I need to do it. I wouldn't care if you had a million dollars in the bank, I'd still want to give this to you."

"If I had a million dollars in the bank we would've never met."

Mozart just brought Summer's hand up to his lips and kissed the back of it. Then he turned it over and nipped the fleshy part of her palm. "Come on, Sunshine, we've got some rooms to clean."

"YOU'RE REALLY GOOD at this," Summer told Mozart honestly when they were working on the last room for the day.

"I don't mean to be a dick, but it's really not that hard, Sunshine."

Summer laughed. "Sorry, you're right."

"Besides, I'm single. I have to clean my own apartment and the Navy made sure I could make a bed so tight, a quarter would bounce off the sheets."

Summer laughed again. "Obviously a good life-skill to have." She smiled at Mozart. He'd made the job of cleaning the rooms fun. They'd talked while they'd cleaned and she'd gotten to know him a bit better. Summer learned he had a wicked sense of humor. Mozart could laugh at himself as well as make her see humor in situations that she might not have seen otherwise. Overall she really enjoyed spending time with him.

Summer stopped and stood still for a moment and looked at him. "Thank you, Mozart."

Mozart heard the seriousness of Summer's tone and turned to her. "For what?"

"For helping me today. For not freaking out about having to clean toilets or make beds or vacuum floors. For everything. Just...thank you."

Mozart dropped the bundle of dirty towels he'd been carrying to the cart, and took Summer's head in his hands and rested his forehead against hers. "You're welcome."

They looked into each other's eyes for a beat, until Summer pulled away and looked away feeling awkward.

"Look at me, Sunshine," Mozart ordered.

Summer immediately looked up into his eyes, not even questioning why she'd immediately done what he'd asked.

"Don't ever feel embarrassed for telling me what's on your mind. If you're pissed, tell me. If you're happy, I want to know. If you're embarrassed, tired, hungry, sad...I want to know. Got me?"

Without breaking eye contact, Summer simply nodded.

"Okay then. Let's finish cleaning this shithole and grab something to eat then get to the store. I'm in the mood to spoil you."

"Okay."

Cleaning the rest of the room took no time at all and soon they were stashing the cart in the back of the office building and the cleaning supplies in the storage room.

"Come on, Sunshine, let's go. We have crap to buy."

"I hope you know I'm not going to let you go overboard."

"Yeah, yeah, let's go."

SUMMER SAT ON the edge of the bed and looked around in bemusement. Mozart had gone overboard. Nothing she'd said made any difference. He'd just ignored her protests and bought whatever he wanted to. There was a small microwave now sitting beside the television set. A dorm-room size refrigerator now stood, motor running, against the wall and there was food everywhere. Mozart had bought so much food, it was stacked around the room haphazardly. The small fridge was overflowing with enough food to keep her fed for at least two weeks.

Summer could tell Mozart was in a weird mood while they were shopping, so she hadn't protested what he'd thrown in to the cart after the first time she'd tried. He'd turned to her and said gruffly, "Let me do this, Sunshine. I *need* to do this." So she'd let Mozart do what it was he felt he needed to.

He'd sent her to the clothes section of the store and ordered her to find long sleeved shirts and pants, a jacket, and even underwear in her size. Mozart had threatened if she didn't come back with what he thought was enough, *he'd* then go and find clothes for her. Summer took him at his word and brought back what she'd thought was way too many clothes. Mozart had only sighed and let it go with a, "that'll do for now."

Now they were in the room, and Summer felt awkward. She wasn't used to anyone buying her things, well buying her things because she couldn't afford it. She didn't like the feeling. Mozart sat next to her on the edge of the bed and she saw him staring at the food they'd brought in.

"I don't know if that'll be enough," he said morose-ly.

"Are you kidding?"

"No," Mozart said in a flat voice, turning to her. "We're headed out on a mission on Monday. I have no idea how long I'll be gone, and I don't know when I'll be able to get back up here again. I know you don't have a car so you can't just run to the store to get anything if you run out."

Summer put her hand on Mozart's leg, then snatched it back when he flinched. Before she could say or do anything, he grabbed her hand and put it back on his leg. Mozart tilted his head in an invitation for her to say what it was she obviously wanted to say.

"I'm not saying this to make you feel guilty, or mad, or anything, okay?" When Mozart nodded, Summer continued. "Mozart, for the last few months I've been eating one meal a day. When Henry opens the office I head over there and eat a yogurt and a bagel. I typically snatch another bagel and a piece of fruit for later. Sometimes a guest will leave something in their room that I feel is safe to take for myself to eat. Trust me, all of this food…" She gestured around them, "…will last me a good long time."

Summer watched as Mozart's left hand curled into a fist and the muscle in his jaw clenched. Not wanting him to torture himself, she brought the hand not resting on his leg, up to his face and turned it toward her. Whispering, Summer said, "I'm okay, Mozart. You have no idea how much what you've done for me in the last two days means to me. If I was okay before, now I'm *more* than okay."

Mozart took a deep breath and turned his head and kissed the palm of Summer's hand. "You'll never have to eat the fucking trash that someone leaves behind again. Just the thought..." he shuddered and closed his eyes for a moment.

Summer could tell when he'd gotten himself back under control. He opened his eyes and told her, "I'll be back up here as soon as I can, Sunshine."

"I know."

"I know you don't have a cell phone, but I'm going to leave you my number so you can call me whenever you want. I'll call you here at the motel to let you know when I'll be back up, but in the meantime, when I'm out of the country, if I give you a friend's number will you call it if you need anything...and I mean anything?"

Summer stayed silent and just looked at Mozart.

"Shit. You won't will you? I knew you were going to be a pain." Mozart smiled when he said it, so Summer wasn't offended. "Will you take the number for my peace of mind then? I'll feel better if you have it."

"Whose number is it?"

"His name is Tex. He's a friend who lives in Virginia. He used to be a SEAL, but was medically retired after having his leg partially amputated. He's a computer genius and I'd trust him with my life…or yours."

"Leave me his number, Mozart. I can't promise to call if I get a splinter or something, but if something goes seriously wrong I'll call." At the look of relief in Mozart's eyes, Summer knew she'd said the right thing, even if it made her uncomfortable.

Mozart stood up and held his hand out to Summer. "Come on, Sunshine. Let's climb in bed, there has to be a movie or something on television we can watch."

Summer took Mozart's hand and he led her to the bed. He didn't pull back the covers, but helped her onto the bed and climbed in behind her. He pointed the remote at the TV and flipped through the channels until he came upon *True Lies*.

"I've always loved this movie. This okay?"

"Yeah, Jamie Lee Curtis kicks butt."

Mozart laughed and settled back against the pillows and drew Summer into his side. She snuggled down against him and put her head against his chest. Mozart took a deep breath and inhaled her scent.

"You smell good." He couldn't have stopped the words to save his life.

"It's just shampoo."

"No, it's not. It's shampoo, and the orange you ate

tonight as a snack when we got back to the room. It's a hint of salt from your perspiration, it's *you* Sunshine."

Summer squirmed. She'd never had anyone talk to her like Mozart did. "You're crazy."

"Take the compliment, Summer. Say thank you."

"Thank you."

Mozart smiled at her and pulled her even closer. "Now, shhhh. Watch the movie."

Summer tried to lose herself in the movie, but couldn't. Her mind was jumping around and she couldn't turn it off. Finally, she tipped her head up to ask Mozart a question, only to find him staring down at her, instead of at the TV.

"You're going on a mission on Monday?"

"Yeah."

"Can you tell me anything about it?" Summer didn't think he could, but asked anyway.

"No." After a minute or two of silence Mozart told her regretfully, "It's what I do, Sunshine."

Summer nodded immediately and tried to reassure him. "Oh, I know, Mozart. I don't know much...okay, I don't know anything about the military, but I know enough to know what you do is kept hush hush and that you can't talk about it. I just...I just will worry about you." She rushed to continue, "I know, it's silly, I don't really even know you, but I don't like thinking about you heading off to some foreign country doing something dangerous and not knowing anything about where you are, what you're doing, or when you'll be back."

Mozart sighed and turned to Summer. He leaned over until she was lying sideways on the bed and he was leaning over her. "I don't like keeping things from you, but you have to know I can never tell you. It's the hardest part of being with a SEAL. I wish I had time to introduce you to Ice, Alabama, and Fiona. They're my teammates' women. They've learned to deal with our missions by getting together and doing girl stuff. We know us leaving drives them crazy, but they support each other and help each other get through it. And you should know, the team knows what we're doing. Yes, what we do is dangerous and there's always the chance we'll be hurt..." Mozart drew a finger over his scarred cheek, then continued, "but you have to believe in us. We've trained for this. We're good, Sunshine. The fact that Wolf, Abe, and Cookie have their women waiting at home for them makes them even more determined that we all come home." He stopped talking and stared down at the amazing woman under him.

"I get it, Mozart. I know you're good. I know you're a professional. But I'll still worry." Summer said the last in a small, unsure voice. "I don't even know why you're here really. I mean, you don't know me..."

"Come here, Sunshine, and listen to me." Mozart lay back on his side and pulled her toward him. They were face to face on the bed, not touching, but close enough to feel each other's breaths as they exhaled in and out.

"You're right in that we haven't spent a lot of time together. If one of my buddies was in this same situation I'd probably be warning him to slow down. I'd tell him that there was no way he could have feelings for you after knowing you two damn days. But, I know my own mind. I see *you*. You're smart. You're compassionate. You're tough. You're selfless. You're hardworking. You're shy. You're passionate. You're beautiful. You're everything I've ever dreamed about in a woman. If you think I'm walking away from you, you're out of your mind. I'm not proposing. I'm not saying we'll be together for the rest of our lives. What I *am* saying that I want to see where this can go. I want to get to know you better. I want to protect you. I want to taste you so badly, I'm practically salivating. So, yeah, I get what you're saying when you say you'll worry, 'cos I'll worry too. I worry about you up here with that asshole, Henry. I worry about you eating enough. I worry about you being cold. I worry about you working too hard. I worry about you not having any transportation. I know we haven't known each other very long, but that worry is there. So while I don't like that you'll worry about me, at the same time, I like it."

"Mozart…" Summer couldn't get anything else out.

She wished she could've taped what he'd just said so she could play it back over and over again.

"Any other concerns about us not knowing each other or why I'm here?"

Summer could only shake her head.

Mozart smiled. "Then can we finish watching Arnold kick the bad guys' butts?"

"Yeah, we can do that."

"A pain in my ass." Mozart leaned toward Summer and kissed her. He didn't touch her with any other part of his body, only his lips.

After a long intense kiss that left them both breathless, Mozart sat up against the headboard again and pulled Summer back into his arms. They watched the movie until the credits rolled across the screen.

Mozart kissed the top of Summer's head and said, "Ready for bed?"

"Yeah," she sleepily muttered.

"Up you go, Sunshine. Go and do your thing." Mozart helped Summer up and gently pushed her toward the bathroom. "I'll change and switch places with you after you're done."

Summer nodded and shuffled into the bathroom. By the time she finished brushing her teeth, washing her face, and using the restroom, Mozart had changed into a T-shirt and was wearing a pair of black boxers. She swallowed hard. "Your turn."

Mozart walked toward her and leaned down and kissed her hard before scooting by. "Mint toothpaste. I've dreamed about that taste on your lips as well," and he disappeared into the bathroom.

Summer hurried into the new pajamas he'd bought for her. Not being the nightgown type, she'd chosen a shorts and mini-tee set. They were loose and pink with little white flowers. She didn't think it was too revealing, but everything seemed very intimate with Mozart.

She was still standing by the bed when he came out of the bathroom. Mozart stopped in his tracks and just stared at her.

Not able to stand the silence and the weird look on his face another moment Summer asked, "What?"

"Get in bed, Sunshine. Now."

Confused, and feeling vulnerable, Summer scurried to the bed and got in. She watched as Mozart came around the side of the bed that she was lying on and said, "Scoot over, I'm on this side."

She'd forgotten. She'd crawled into the side of the bed closest to the door without thinking. Summer scooted over and watched as Mozart leaned over and turned off the light next to the bed. The room plunged into darkness. She felt Mozart settle onto the mattress. Summer waited, but he didn't turn toward her. It felt like he was lying as stiff as a board.

"Mozart?"

"Don't." Mozart cut her off.

Summer was so confused. She had no idea what had happened between when he kissed her and commented on the taste of her toothpaste and when he'd come out of the bathroom. She rolled over so her back was to him and tried to keep her tears from falling.

After a moment, Summer felt Mozart finally move. He turned into her and curled himself around her back. One arm went under her neck, and the other curled over her side and he laid his forearm along her breast-bone. She felt protected and safe in his arms. She was so confused.

"Don't cry, Sunshine. Fuck. I'm sorry. You are so gorgeous. Seeing you standing there in that cute little sleep set almost made me lose control. It took every-thing I had to let you climb in here by yourself. I still want nothing more than to turn you over and bury myself so far inside you that you'll never forget the feel of me. But I promised. It's too soon. Jesus, Sunshine, don't ever doubt that I want to be here with you. I just needed a moment to control myself."

Summer could feel Mozart's hard length against her. She didn't doubt him, but he'd hurt her. "Don't do that again," she sniffed once, hard. "I thought you'd changed your mind. I can't take up and down emotions directed at me. I need you to be one person. If you're mad, tell me. If you're stressed, tell me. If you're losing control, tell me. I know with what you do you'll probably have some moments where you're dealing with some heavy stuff. I'll give you the space you need, but if you don't tell me, I'll think it's about me." She shrugged as best she could in his embrace. It was easier to talk to him since she wasn't looking at him. "I'm a woman. We tend to think *everything's* about us."

"I will. I'm sorry."

There it was. He laid it out straight. He didn't make excuses or try to blow off what she'd said. She sighed and snuggled into his arms.

"Thank you."

"Sleep, Sunshine. Tomorrow we'll go back to the diner and have another way too big breakfast, we'll drive to the overlook and do the touristy thing downtown. We'll clean the damn rooms and then we'll go out for dinner. I have to leave after we eat, but I want to spend every moment I can with you before I go."

"I want that too."

"Sleep."

"I'm glad you're here, Mozart."

"Me too. There's nowhere I'd rather be. I just wish I'd gotten here sooner."

"Don't. You're here now."

"Yes, I'm here now. Now…sleep woman."

Summer giggled. He was so demanding, but she loved it. She couldn't resist trying to get the last word in. "I'd sleep if someone stopped talking to me."

Mozart growled. "Don't make me turn you over my knee, Sunshine."

"You wouldn't!"

"Try me."

Summer giggled again and wiggled in Mozart's arms until she'd turned over and was now facing him. She could feel his erection pressed up against her. She squirmed closer to him and buried her head in his neck.

Whispering, she told him, "I'll try anything you want to do, Mozart."

"Good God, woman. You're pushing me. Now hush. Have some pity on your SEAL. Go. To. Sleep."

Summer fell asleep feeling safe and warm for only the second time in months, the first being the night before. She didn't know that Mozart stayed awake for hours watching her sleep and counting his lucky stars he'd come back up the mountain for her when he did.

Chapter Ten

A FTER ANOTHER HUGE breakfast, they made their way back to the motel to clean the rooms. Summer was amazed how quickly the job went with two people doing it. Mozart was right, it wasn't hard, but it was tedious. Not all of the guests were slobs, but enough were that it made the job annoying and, at times, disgusting.

Mozart made the job, if not fun, bearable. He took over the making of the beds and cleaning the toilets, while she was in charge of the dirty linen, the cleaning and vacuuming. The first time she'd bent over to tuck in a sheet, Mozart had made a noise in the back of his throat that sounded a lot like a growl and had pulled her upright.

"I'll do that. There's no way I can watch you bend over bed after bed and not throw you down on one of them, Sunshine."

Just the memory of the way he'd growled the words at her in his low rumbly voice, made goose bumps break out over Summer's body.

She'd just smiled at him and agreed.

Now the cleaning was done and they were sitting on a bench overlooking the lake. It was chilly, and Mozart had one arm wrapped around Summer's shoulders. The area was quiet. Winter wasn't the most popular time for people to hang out at the lake. They were usually up in the mountains skiing.

"Penny for your thoughts," Summer said, breaking the comfortable silence.

"I'm thinking about how if I didn't get my head out of my ass and get up here when I did, you'd be sleeping basically outside all winter."

Summer turned and kissed Mozart's jaw then rested her head on his shoulder with her face turned toward his neck. "If it got too bad, I would've said something."

"Would you?"

Summer sat up and sighed. "Yes, Mozart. I might be down on my luck, but I'm not a complete idiot. Henry's an ass, but even he wouldn't have made me sleep in that thing if there was a foot of snow on the ground. Besides, Joseph was working on making it more like a guest room than a storage room."

"Joseph? Who the hell is that?"

"He's the new handyman. I told you about him."

Mozart snorted. "I can't believe someone else knew you were living in that shithole and didn't say anything."

The silence stretched between them. Mozart finally broke it.

"I want to have Ice or one of the other women call you while we're gone. Will you talk to them?"

"Why?"

"We talked about this a little bit yesterday. They're each other's support while we're gone. I want you to have that."

"But they don't know me, Mozart. They aren't going to want to talk to me about that stuff."

"They will."

Summer just shook her head. She knew better. "Okay, whatever you want, Mozart."

Mozart turned on the bench and put his hands on Summer's shoulders. His thumbs rubbed against her collarbone. He knew she wouldn't be able to feel it through her clothes and jacket, but the motion soothed him. Hell, anytime he touched her soothed him. "I've been told that when a woman says 'whatever,' they usually mean anything but. What's wrong, Sunshine?"

Summer sighed and avoided Mozart's eyes. She looked past him to the trail that meandered around the lake. "It just won't work, Mozart. You can't go to your friends and tell them you've met a woman and would they please call, make friends, and talk about their feelings of worry about their men. It doesn't work that way. Hell, I had people I knew for *years* not bother to call me to see how I was doing after my divorce and losing my job. For all your catting around, you don't know much about women."

"Look at me."

Summer sighed and brought her eyes back to Mozart's. She could see he was concerned and frustrated. His eyebrows were drawn down and his forehead was wrinkled in stress lines. Even the scar on his face seemed to be redder than normal.

"I want you to get to know them. I want them to get to know you. I don't want you up here alone. Everything in me is rebelling against it."

"I've been alone a long time. This isn't anything I haven't been through before."

"But you're not alone anymore. You have me."

Summer's eyes teared up and she bit her lip.

Mozart tugged her lip out of her teeth and leaned forward. "Let me try, please? If one of them does call, will you talk to her? Will you give their friendship a try?"

"Of course I will. I miss having someone to talk to, but I don't want you to go back home and browbeat them into calling me. If you're as much as a flirt as you've told me you were, if you've slept with as many women as your reputation warrants, they're going to think I'm just another woman in your long line of conquests."

"They won't."

"They *will*, Mozart. Jeez, we've been through this. I'm a woman. I know these things. You'll go down there and say, 'Hey, I met a woman up at Big Bear, while we're gone will you please call her and include her in your tight clique of friends?' and they're going to agree, because they like you and you're their friend, but when push comes to shove, I'm a stranger. To them, I'm just another woman you've picked up."

"You're wrong."

Pulling away, Summer stood up and stalked two steps away from the bench and Mozart and faced the lake with her arms around her stomach. "Shit, Mozart. I'm not wrong."

Summer felt his arms come around her chest from behind.

Mozart put his head on Summer's shoulder and squeezed her tight. His lips went to her ear and he spoke low and earnestly.

"I have never asked Ice or the others to talk to any of the women I 'picked up.' Those women were gone from my life the second I left their bed. I've never seen any of them more than once. I know this is hard for you to understand, but Ice is just like you. She's loyal to a fault. She was there when those assholes carved into my face. She *knows* me. I'm not going to go to her and tell her I met a woman. I'm going to go to her and tell her I met *my* woman. As soon as the words leave my mouth, she'll be hounding me to give her your phone number. Trust me, Sunshine. I won't leave you hanging again. If I tell you she'll call, she'll call."

Summer felt herself being turned and she buried her face in Mozart's chest. She felt his arm go around and rest in the small of her back. His other hand went to the back of her neck and he held her to him. She clutched his jacket in her hands that were wedged between their bodies.

"I need this, Sunshine. I need to know you have my friends at your back. I swear after talking to them once, they'll be your friends too. They won't leave you hanging. They'll follow up on the friendship. I swear it."

"Okay, Mozart. I trust you. I'll talk to her if she calls."

"*When* she calls."

Summer smiled, despite her emotional state. "When she calls."

"Jesus, you're a pain in my ass." Mozart pulled away and looked down at Summer. Her nose and the tips of her ears were red with the cold and she had no make-up on, but she was the most beautiful woman he'd ever seen. She wasn't afraid to argue with him. She wasn't afraid to tell him exactly what she was thinking, and she wanted him to tell her what he was thinking. She was perfect. "You're mine, Sunshine. I'll be back up here as soon as I can. Just please remember that my friends are your friends now. Okay?"

"Okay."

"Let's get out of the cold and go grab something to eat."

Summer let Mozart lead them back toward his truck. The day was going by too fast. He'd be leaving soon. Way too soon.

DINNER WENT BY quickly. No matter how much Summer tried to ignore the elephant in the room, she couldn't. Mozart was leaving. He'd done so much for her in the short time he'd been back, it almost felt like it was happening to someone else. Summer wasn't naïve. She knew Mozart was controlling and her situation was as out of control as it could get. She hoped he'd feel the same way about her when he got back from wherever it was he was going, but she couldn't be sure. She'd have to play it by ear.

They left the restaurant and made their way back to the motel. Mozart grabbed her hand and led her into room seven without a word. When they were back inside the room he finally dropped her hand and went over the little desk. He tore a piece of paper off the pad of paper there and wrote on it. Then he went over to the phone sitting next to the bed and wrote the phone number listed there on another piece of paper, which he shoved into his pocket.

Mozart came back over to where Summer was standing, and took her hand again. He led her to the end of the bed and they sat down. He sat sideways, as he had only two short nights ago, and kept her hand in his.

"Okay, Sunshine. Here are the numbers I told you about. Tex is my friend in Virginia. I've also written down my cell, home, and work number. Ice's number is here as well. I would've given you Fiona and Alabama's too, but I know you well enough to know it will be a stretch for you to call any of the numbers I've given you. Just please, promise me you'll call me or Tex or Ice if you need anything."

"I'm not going to need anything, Mozart."

"You don't know that. Anything can happen at the drop of a hat."

"It won't."

"Seriously, listen to me. I'm going to tell you something that only my fellow SEALs know. I'm not sure if they've even told their women."

Summer could only nod. He was drop dead serious. She'd never seen Mozart look so anxious and concerned.

"I thought the same way you do once. I was a teenager, living my life. We were happy, we were normal. Then my little sister was kidnapped. She was gone for over two weeks. We had no idea where she was. A couple found her beaten body in the woods. She'd been sexually assaulted and strangled. She didn't deserve it. We didn't think anything bad would ever happen either. I *know* bad things can happen, Summer. I've lived through it. Please…for me. Promise, if anything happens you'll call. If I can't be in the country to help you, I need to know you'll reach out. Tex can help you."

"I promise." Summer didn't even pause. It was obvious Mozart needed this from her. She couldn't imagine how he and his family had made it through something like that, but it explained a lot about him.

Mozart let out a breath he wasn't aware he'd been holding.

"I promise, Mozart," Summer said again, putting her hand on his scarred cheek.

"Thank you." Mozart pulled Summer into his arms and they sat on the bed holding each other for a long moment.

"This sucks."

Summer had to laugh. It did suck, but Mozart sounded like a petulant little boy. She pulled back. "Don't be such a baby. You'll be back before you know it. I'll be here doing the same thing day after day. I have the gazillion phone numbers you gave me. People have long-distance relationships all the time."

"I don't."

"Well, I'm not sure you count. Have you ever even had a relationship before?"

"Well, no. But it still sucks."

Summer smiled. "I don't know how this happened so fast. It's crazy. But I'm going to miss you."

"You better."

They smiled at each other.

"I have to get going. We have to meet at the base early in the morning." Mozart said the words, but didn't move.

"Will you kiss me before you go?"

"As if you have to ask. Come here." Mozart pulled Summer back into his arms and fell sideways on the bed clutching her to him. He put his hand on the back of her head and pulled her to him. There was no tenderness in his kiss. He controlled her, he inhaled her. He devoured her.

Mozart's other hand caressed her back, then her side, then went down to the hem of her T-shirt. As he kissed her, Mozart pulled up her shirt until he was touching her warm skin and slowly ran his hand up her side until he'd reached her breast.

He re-angled his head and rolled until Summer was underneath him. He put one of his legs in between hers and held her in place. He felt her other leg pull up until her foot rested on the bed and she pushed her knee against his hip. Mozart knew the entire situation was getting out of control, quickly, but he couldn't help himself. He needed to feel her at least once before he left.

He brought his hand to Summer's chest under her shirt and encased her bra covered breast with his hand. Mozart felt her inhale at the same time he felt her nipple go taut under his palm. Wanting to see her eyes when he touched her for the first time, he drew back. Summer's eyes were closed and she arched her back into his touch.

"Open your eyes, Sunshine," Mozart ordered gruffly.

Summer's eyes popped open, they were dilated and she was panting against him.

"Touch me," she begged softly, not breaking eye contact.

Mozart shifted and brought himself closer to her. He could feel her heat through both their clothes, against his hard length. Not looking away from her face, he slowly brought the edge of her bra down until it caught under the curve of her breast. He wished like hell he could see her, but this was almost more erotic. Her T-shirt covered her, but he knew if he looked down he'd see her nipple straining against the fabric.

Finally, he curled his hand over her bare breast. They both inhaled at the same time. Not satisfied, Mozart explored. He ran his fingertips in circles around

Summer's areola, not touching her hardening nipple. He pushed and caressed, all the while staring into her eyes.

After a moment, not being able to stand not touching her fully anymore, he asked, "Ready, Sunshine?"

"Oh God, yes. Please. Touch me."

Not making her beg anymore, Mozart took his thumb and index finger and squeezed her nipple. Summer arched her back and groaned, closing her eyes for the first time since he'd touched her bare skin.

Mozart continued to roll her nipple with his fingertips. "Jesus, you're magnificent. You're perfect. I can't wait to see these beauties. You're so responsive. When I finally get you naked underneath me I don't think we're going to come up for air for days."

"Yes, oh God, *yes*."

Mozart leaned down and took her nipple in his mouth through her T-shirt. This was further than he was planning on taking this, but he couldn't help himself. Summer was so sexy and so open. He sucked as hard as he could through the cotton of her shirt and was rewarded with another agonized moan from her. Mozart could feel her squirming under him.

Knowing they were both almost too far gone to stop, Mozart took her nipple in his teeth and lightly tugged. Finally, he brought his head up to look at Summer's face and saw she was watching him.

"That is sexy as hell," she told him honestly, once again laying it out for him with no artifice.

"No, you're sexy as hell," he responded, all the while still rolling her nipple in his hand.

After a long moment, Mozart stilled and covered her breast with his large hand regretfully. He laid his forehead on her shoulder. He felt one of her hands come up and rest on the back of his head. He vaguely remembered her nails digging into his back while he'd been feasting on her nipple, but couldn't be sure.

"The second we land, I'm on my way up here. I'm done giving you time." It wasn't a question.

"Okay."

Mozart raised his head and told Summer seriously. "You're mine. I've never almost come from sucking a woman's tits through her shirt before. I have no idea what it is about you, but all I know is that you're mine."

"Uh...that wasn't the most romantic thing I've ever heard, but..."

"I'm not usually a romantic guy, Summer, but with you, I want to be. I can feel how hot you are through our clothes. If you think I'm going to spend another night lying beside you and not feeling that heat on my skin, you're crazy. You're fucking mine." Mozart wanted so badly to order her to come to Riverton with him, but knew he couldn't.

"I've never come just from...that...before either."

Mozart did a double take. "You…"

"Yeah."

"Jesus. A pain in my ass." Mozart smiled when he said it, but felt ten feet tall. "If that's all it takes, we're going to have a hell of a good time when I get back."

"It's you. Your smell. The growly sounds you make. The way you take charge. The way your hands feel against my skin. The way you look into my eyes. It's just *you*."

Mozart's hand still rested again her skin and Summer could feel it clench in reaction to her words. Her nipple immediately peaked again.

Reluctantly, Mozart took his hand from her breast and pulled her bra up to cover her again. He ran his hand sensuously down her stomach and over until it rested on her hipbone. "You're too skinny. The next time I see you I want some meat on your bones."

"Okay."

"And if you run out of food, you call Tex, he'll take care of it."

"Okay."

"And I want you to call me every day while I'm gone. Leave me a message so I know you're all right."

"I don't have any money to make long distance calls." Summer was honest with him.

"I'll leave a calling card for you."

"But, you won't even get the messages if you're out

of the country."

"Sunshine…"

"Okay, okay. Bossy. I will."

"And please, God, lock this door and stay safe."

"Okay."

"I gotta go."

"I know."

"I'll be back."

"Okay."

"*I'll be back.*"

"I *know.*"

"Kiss me one more time before I go."

"WOLF? THIS IS MOZART. Can I talk to Ice?" The second Mozart pulled out of the parking lot of the *Big Bear Cabins* and away from Summer, he picked up his cell and called Wolf. He needed to talk to Ice now.

"Everything all right?"

Mozart knew Wolf would protect Caroline from any danger, emotional or physical. He didn't get pissed. Mozart knew Wolf was just protecting his woman. For the first time in his life he got it. He felt the same way about Summer. Mozart didn't even give Wolf any crap about it, just answered, "Yeah, everything is okay. I just need a favor."

"Hang on."

Mozart waiting impatiently, drumming his fingers on the steering wheel as he headed down out of the mountains. He had no idea how much it would hurt to leave Summer. Everything was so up in the air and he hated it. Hell, he hadn't even slept with her and he couldn't imagine not seeing her every day. He had it bad.

"Hey, Sam, what's up?"

Mozart didn't think he'd ever get used to be calling Sam, but for Ice, he didn't complain.

"I need you to expand your posse during this mission."

"My posse?"

"Yeah, your group. You know, you girls get together and support each other while we're gone."

"I don't understand."

"I met someone. I'd like for you to call her while we're gone. Make sure she's okay. You know…include her. She'll worry like you guys will, and I'd like for her to have a support system."

"You met someone?"

"Yeah."

"You *met* someone?"

"Yeah, Ice. What the hell?"

"Hold on."

Mozart actually took the phone away from his ear and looked at the screen in confusion for a second. He knew this would be weird, but Ice was acting even stranger than he thought she would. He smiled a second later when he heard Ice let out a muffled screech in the background then exclaim, "It's about time!" She sounded completely calm and composed when she came back on the phone. "What's her name?"

Mozart chuckled. "I told Summer you'd act like this."

"Summer? That's her name?"

"Yeah."

"And you told her you'd be calling me and I'd be excited that you'd met someone?"

"Not exactly in those words, but yeah."

"I like her already."

"You'll like her. But, Ice, she's got some hang-ups…" Before he could continue Caroline interrupted him.

"Who doesn't?"

"I just mean, I told her you'd call her. If you don't…it'll destroy her."

"Don't worry, Sam, I'll call her."

Not able to keep the relief out of his voice Mozart said, "Thank you."

"Now tell me everything."

"Everything?"

"Yeah, how you met, where she works, what's going on…you know…everything."

Mozart chuckled. When Ice got her mind set on something, there was no shaking her. At least it'd make the drive back to Riverton interesting.

By the time Mozart pulled into the parking lot at his apartment complex he felt a lot better about leaving Summer. He still wasn't happy about it, but he knew Ice and the other women would take care of her for him until he could get back. He'd have to live with it until he could convince her to move down and to live with him. The thought of her living with him didn't even freak him out. She was his. Period. *But,* the thought of her needing him when he wasn't there, *did* freak him out. He knew it stemmed from Avery's kidnapping and feeling helpless in the aftermath, but it was what it was.

He'd been honest with Summer that the thought of her being cold or hungry made him crazy. He knew all the times he'd made fun of Wolf or Abe or Cookie while they'd been on a mission would come back to haunt him. He knew now why they felt so anxious when they were away from their women. He felt it now. They were protectors at heart and being in a position where they *couldn't* protect their women, was not a good feeling.

Chapter Eleven

Hey, Mozart, it's me. For the record, again, I think it's silly that you ordered me to leave you a message every day. What if your message space gets used up and someone important needs to leave you a message? Anyway, nothing is going on here. The guest load has still been light, so that's good for me. Henry is as ornery as ever. Not sure what's up his butt, but he's leaving me alone. I still have ten tons of food to eat, so that's all good. Joseph has been working on upgrading the rooms a bit. Apparently the fridge and microwave in the room thing that you did for me made Henry think, and he's putting one in every room. Not sure it'll help bring people in, but it's something. Joseph has also been trying to spruce up the grounds to make them look better. Today he started painting some of the unused rooms. He's been a great help around here. Anyway, I hope you're all right and your...thing...is going okay. I miss you. Bye.

S UMMER HUNG UP the phone. It really was ridiculous that Mozart wanted her to leave a message every day, but she couldn't deny it gave her goose bumps to think of him listening to all of them when he got back. It was like she was leaving a diary of her days and it was intimate. Even if it was only a message.

She didn't really have anything interesting to tell him though, and Summer worried about that. Her life was pretty boring. She didn't have a car, so she just hung around the motel all the time. But at least now she was warm and wasn't constantly hungry.

She hadn't heard from Mozart's friend though. She didn't really expect it, no matter what he'd told her, but it still hurt. It reminded her of how she felt when she'd first met Mozart. He'd said he'd come back and hadn't. Even though Summer didn't think he was serious, a part of her, deep down, believed him. He'd been so earnest when he'd told her that this Ice person would call, he'd made her believe. Now, four days had gone by and her phone hadn't rung once.

Summer loved being able to skip breakfast in the office. She'd always hated how Henry glared at her when she'd taken extra food to eat later. Now that Mozart had set her up, she didn't have to worry about it. She was able to sleep in and get ready leisurely in her room. This morning she didn't have as much time as usual, however, because Henry told her they had a few more people than usual checking in that day. Check-in was typically three o'clock, but this group had requested an earlier arrival time. It wouldn't have been a big deal, but because Joseph was painting some of the rooms, they didn't have as many to rent out. Summer had to start work earlier than usual in order to get the rooms ready. It wasn't a big group, only three rooms, but Henry was desperate for whatever business he could get, so he was acting as if they were about to entertain the queen of England or something.

Summer had just closed the door to the last room she had to clean for the day when she heard a car drive into the small parking lot. She glanced over as she headed toward the storage building to put away her cleaning supplies and to stow the cart, and saw three women climb out of a big-ass SUV. The vehicle looked new and it was huge. Summer knew she'd never be comfortable driving something like that around. She just shrugged and continued on her way. She couldn't wait to crash in her room. She was tired and a bit depressed. She missed Mozart more than she thought she would and she just wanted to watch TV and veg for a bit.

As she was walking back to her room, the three ladies came out of the office. Summer looked over at them and was shocked when one called out her name. Summer stopped and turned to look at them. They were now walking toward her. Summer clasped her jacket more firmly around her. When guests talked to her, it always made her nervous. She was adamant about turning in anything that was left in the rooms, but it was inevitable that one would eventually accuse her of stealing something they'd misplaced themselves. Summer didn't recognize these women, but that didn't mean they didn't remember what she looked like. She was the only maid at the motel.

"Yes?" The word came out a bit harsher than Summer intended, but it was too late to take it back.

"You are Summer right? Sam's Summer?"

"Sam?"

One of the other women laughed. "Mozart. Caroline means Mozart."

Summer could only stare at the women in confusion. "Uh, I know Mozart if that's what you're getting at." Were these some of Mozart's previous conquests? She felt completely in the dark.

"Shit, you guys, you're scaring her. Summer, I'm Fiona. That's Caroline and Alabama. Did Sam tell you about us?"

Summer was floored. She thought Caroline was going to call her. Not show up here, and not with anyone else in tow. She nervously smoothed a strand of hair behind her ear. "He said you'd call me." She said bluntly, looking at the woman called Caroline.

"I know. He phoned the minute he left here on Sunday and asked if I'd call you. But I talked with Fee and Alabama and we decided we should take a road trip. We wanted to meet the woman who brought Sam to heel, and we also wanted to do what he wanted us to—reassure you about our men. That they know what they're doing and that they'll be back in one piece."

Summer still didn't know what to say. She felt completely awkward. "O-kaaaay."

Caroline laughed and took a step forward and linked her arm with Summer's as if she'd known her for years, rather than minutes. "I know, I sound like a crazy lady. But I swear I'm not." She looked at Summer with a seriousness she hadn't shown before. "You've caught Sam's eye. That doesn't happen. Ever. So when he told me he was worried about you and he wanted me to give you a call, I knew we'd be coming up here. You're one of us. Being with a SEAL isn't an easy thing. In fact there are times when it down-right sucks. So we wanted to come up here and show you our support. We have to stick together. So how about it?"

"Are you staying here?"

Alabama spoke up for the first time, "It's not exactly the Ritz is it?"

"Uh. No. I'm sure you guys could find a better place than this."

"Yeah, but this is where you are. So here we are."

Fiona said bluntly. "Come on, Summer. What do you have to lose to spend some time with us? Are we so bad?"

Horrified these women might think for a second that she didn't want to spend time with them, that she wasn't excited to have them here, Summer quickly sputtered, "Oh no. God. No, I'm thrilled you guys are here. I just don't really understand why, but I'm still thrilled. Anyone that is Mozart's friend, I hope is my friend too."

"Are you done for the day?" Caroline asked.

Summer nodded.

"Good. Let us get settled then we'll go and see what trouble we can get into. We're hungry."

"Okay. Meet back here in fifteen minutes? Is that enough time for you guys?" Fiona asked the group in general. Everyone agreed and scattered to their rooms. Summer stood in the parking lot for a moment before shaking her head and heading toward her room. She wasn't sure what was in store for her tonight, but whatever it was would be interesting.

SUMMER THREW HER head back and laughed hysterically. These women were hilarious. She couldn't remember a time when she'd had this much fun. They'd met back in the parking lot and all crawled into the monstrous

SUV. Caroline had laughed and said that Matthew had bought it for her because he wanted her to be safe. It sounded very familiar to Summer.

They'd eaten dinner at the same steak place Mozart had taken her to when he'd first met her, then they'd moved their little party to a run-down little shack of a bar. Fiona wasn't drinking, but the rest of them proceeded to down drink after drink. It was fun to be able to let loose for the first time in a long time. Summer wasn't sure she'd feel comfortable enough with these women to let down her inhibitions, but she quickly decided she trusted them enough to get a bit tipsy.

"Do you guys remember when we all went out that one night and the guys followed us and sat in the corner glaring at every man who even looked at us? The manager was so glad when we finally decided to call it a night. I think he was afraid our SEALs would unleash hell on the other patrons and he'd never be able to recoup his losses." The women recounted story after story of their men being protective and bad ass, and they'd done it with a laugh. None of them minded their men's actions.

Seeing Summer's confusion with their stories, Fiona tried to explain, "Summer, being with a SEAL is a balancing act. They're taught from the first time they set foot in boot camp that they are there to protect others. Their teammates, women, other countries, the abused and neglected…it's a part of who they are. While you and I both know we can navigate this world without someone constantly looking over us, they can't get it through their thick skulls. We just have to learn to manage it. We allow them to follow us around when we go out because the rewards outweigh the irritation tenfold."

"What do you mean?"

"Hunter will do anything for me. All I have to do is ask. He will make sure no one harasses me. He'll put aside anything and everything, and has, just to see to me. When you're sad, they'll want to make you happy. When you're happy, they want to know what's causing it so they can make it happen over and over again. And the sex. Whew. I'm assuming you know this, but the sex is out of this world. I never thought in a million years that I'd ever be able to enjoy sex again after what happened to me, but having Hunter focus completely on my satisfaction in bed is something I'll protect and nurture with everything in me."

Feeling the effects of the alcohol, Summer didn't filter her words as she normally would. She could sense something was different about Fiona but didn't know what. "After what happened to you?"

Fiona put one of her hands over Summer's. "Yeah, I'll tell you the whole story someday, but quick version is that I was kidnapped and taken to Mexico to be a part of a sex slave ring. Hunter and the team came down to save someone else, and found me too."

Summer was appalled. She'd read about those sorts of things happening, but had never dreamed she'd meet someone who'd actually survived it. "What?" she shrieked, standing up suddenly, knocking her stool to the floor with a clatter. "Are you shitting me? Did they get them?"

Fiona didn't even look alarmed at her reaction. "Sit back down, Summer, I'm okay. See? I'm here, I'm talking to you. I'm fine. They didn't catch them, but I don't care. Hunter saved me. That's what I'm trying to tell you. I love that he watches over me. I love that he's concerned about me. I'll take his overprotectiveness any day of the week over living through what I did again."

Summer sat down, tears in her eyes. She looked at the other women suddenly, noticing finally that they had been quiet. "What about you guys?" she demanded urgently. "Did that happen to you too?"

"Sam didn't tell you anything about us? Really?" Caroline asked curiously, not answering her question.

"No, now tell me. I can't stand this." Summer rubbed her chest.

"I saved Matthew's life, then he saved mine back after I was kidnapped by terrorists," Caroline said simply.

"I met Christopher when we were at a party and the

building caught fire," Alabama said quietly.

"Are you guys serious? Really?" At their nods she continued. "Oh man, I'm so screwed. I'm so boring compared to you guys. I can't save anyone. I haven't done anything. I'm so normal it isn't even funny."

Fiona leaned toward Summer again. "But don't you see? It doesn't matter. You caught his eye. I think you know that Sam doesn't 'do' relationships. Ever. The fact that he wanted Caroline to call you and bring you into our circle says everything. You obviously don't have to do anything. You being you is what caught his eye."

Slurping the last of her sugary drink out of the bottom of her glass, Summer looked up and muttered, "What if Mozart thinks I'm boring in bed?"

Caroline was the first to react. "Are you saying that you haven't slept with him yet?"

"No, we've slept. But he didn't want to...you know. He said he wanted to wait. I don't know why. Maybe because he doesn't like me that way?" Summer didn't really believe what she was saying. She'd known Mozart was aroused when they'd messed around on the bed before he'd left. It was obvious he wanted her, but he hadn't taken the opportunity. She needed another woman's opinion.

"That proves it, Summer," Caroline said earnestly, sounding much more sober than she was. "If Sam hasn't made love to you yet, he's yours. You don't get it, and

I'm sure you probably don't want to hear this, but he's slept with a lot of women. A lot. And they all meant nothing to him. Hell, he probably couldn't tell you any of their names." At the look of disappointment on Summer's face, she hurried to make her point. "He's never held back, not once. If he's with you, it means you mean something to him. Hell, it means you mean everything to him. He's not a man that goes out of his way to spare the feelings of the women he sleeps with. Don't you get it? It's because he hasn't slept with you that shows how much he cares."

Feeling much more vulnerable than she wanted to, Summer asked quietly, "Are you sure?"

"Oh yeah. I'm sure," Caroline said vehemently.

A smile came over Summer's face. "I like him too."

The other women whooped and laughed. Summer was so happy they'd come up to see her. She felt so much better about Mozart being away. She wasn't going to be happy to see the women leave, but hopefully they'd stay in touch. For the first time in a long time, Summer thought they just might.

After another hour of laughing, drinking, and talking, they decided to call it a night. The four women stumbled their way out of the bar, holding on to Fiona, who was the only sober one, as tight as they could so they wouldn't fall. Giggling and laughing they crawled into the huge SUV and told racy stories all the way back to the motel.

After pulling into an empty spot in front of their rooms, Fiona helped the others out of the huge car. She walked each woman to her room and admonished each one to lock the door. They made plans to get together the next day for lunch, knowing they wouldn't be up for breakfast. Summer knew she'd have to get up and work, but at the moment she didn't care. Fiona came to Summer's door last.

Summer stood in the doorway waiting for Fiona to come and say good night. While waiting she looked over and saw Joseph standing at the end of the row of rooms. Summer had no idea where he'd been staying, but assumed Henry had let him stay in one of the motel rooms just like she was. She half raised her hand to wave at the handyman and watched as he smiled at her and lifted his chin in greeting. Joseph continued to stand there watching, as Fiona secured her friends in their rooms for the night.

"Who's that?"

Summer turned at Fiona's question. "It's just Joseph. He's the handyman around here. He's done a lot of work to make this place look better."

"He's creepy."

Summer looked back to where Joseph had been standing, he wasn't there anymore. She shrugged. "Nah, he's harmless. He's just a loner." Changing the subject she said, "Thank you for coming up here, Fiona. I appreciate it. I know you guys didn't know me and I could've been a bitch."

"We knew you weren't."

"How?" Summer's buzz was wearing off. She wasn't completely sober, but she earnestly wanted to hear what Fiona had to say.

"We heard the story of what you did for Sam when he stayed up here the first time."

"What? How?"

"When he was asking Caroline to call you, he told her the story. He wanted us to know who you were, and it worked. You not caring about Sam's scars was the one sure-fire way to get Caroline to champion you, and Sam knew it. Caroline still feels a lot of guilt for how it happened, even though Sam has told her time and time again that it wasn't her fault. So for you to stand up for him in front of those other women when you didn't even know him? Yeah, that guaranteed she'd be up here. You're one of us now, Summer. We hate it when our men are gone, lying in bed at night worrying about them. We're scared shitless they won't come home. But we never, and I mean never, put that worry on them. We will never tell them how we suffer. They suffer enough in their own way. So we get together and get drunk. We talk to each other about our worries. We need each other, and you need us too. We're a part of a unique club. None of us asked to belong, but here we are. I'm sure you're wondering if it's worth the worry and the dread and the not knowing where they are or what they're doing. I'm telling you it is. It's one hundred percent worth it. These men will do anything for us. For most of us that have been through hell, they're our rocks." Fiona took a breath and leaned toward Summer.

"If you're thinking that you can't handle it, now is the time to break it off. Don't wait. They might act all badass and tough, but deep down they aren't. They're probably more vulnerable than regular men because of what they do. If you need to talk to someone about it, you can always call one of us. We'll be honest with you. But please, don't string Sam along. Don't use him."

Summer relaxed, glad that this was finally coming out. She'd been wondering when it would. She thought it would've come from Caroline though, not Fiona. "I'm glad Mozart has you to look after him. I'm not going to hurt him. I still don't know why he's with me, but I want him." Her words were simple and heartfelt.

Fiona nodded. "Good. Now, get some sleep. We'll see you tomorrow."

"Good night, Fiona. Thanks again."

Summer watched as Fiona went to her room and shut the door behind her. She took one more look around the dark, empty parking lot and saw no one. She shut and locked the door and peeled her clothes off, letting them fall to the ground where she stood and not caring. She hurriedly used the bathroom and brushed her teeth.

Summer pulled a T-shirt over her head and crawled into bed. She reached for the phone. She couldn't resist calling Mozart. She wanted to talk to him so badly she hurt. Leaving a message would have to do.

Hey, it's me. Caroline, Alabama, and Fiona drove up here today. We went out for dinner and had drinks afterwards. Don't worry, Fiona was our sober driver. I like them. I like your friends. I'm so glad you have friends that will look out for you. And just so you know, I like you. I can handle what you do. I can handle your job. If you really want to be with me. I'm here. I can't make it through an hour without remembering everything you've done for me. You've taken care of me without making me feel stifled or weird about it. I like being yours…Shit. I've had too much to drink, so that probably came out wrong, but I just wanted to make sure you knew that I'm not fucking with you. I'm old enough to know what I want, and I'm pretty sure that's you. So, I like your friends. They're funny. I'm not sure they like staying here at the motel, but they did it anyway. Fiona thought Joseph was creepy but I tried to tell her he wasn't, he's just a loner, like I was. But I'm not anymore. I have you. I think I do at least. Okay, now I'm rambling. I have to get up in about five hours but I didn't want to wait to say thank you for calling Caroline. I can't wait to see you again. Bye.

Summer hung up the phone, knowing she sounded like a complete idiot, but hopefully Mozart would figure out what she'd been trying to say. She rolled over and shut her eyes. She was asleep within minutes.

Chapter Twelve

S UMMER WAVED AS the SUV pulled out of the parking lot. She'd spent the last three days with Caroline, Alabama, and Fiona, and was genuinely sad to see them go. They'd certainly opened her eyes about what it was like to be with a man who was a SEAL. She vaguely knew much of what they'd told her, but having them spell it out was eye opening for her.

But nothing they'd said made her want to end it with Mozart. If anything, it made her more determined to be the kind of woman he needed. He worked hard, he risked his life for others, and she wanted to be there when he got home. She wanted to make Mozart's life easier.

Meeting Fiona and knowing she was one of the people Mozart and his team had helped, really brought everything full circle for her. The SEALS went out there, helped other people, and no one knew about it. It was all kept hush-hush. Summer wasn't naïve, she knew they were also sent on missions to kill people. Terrorists, dictators, drug dealers...it didn't matter. She'd put up with Mozart's protective tendencies because she knew for a fact it was how he was made.

The women had one conversation where Summer had wondered out loud if it was her circumstances that made Mozart interested in her. Interested in rescuing her. She'd been quickly disabused of that notion.

Caroline had bluntly told her, "Summer, if that's all it was, don't you think he'd be with someone by now? He's seen hundreds of people like you. Down on their luck, hungry, cold, whatever. He hasn't claimed *them*. He hasn't called us up wanting us to check on *them*. What he's done in the past is contact the authorities, or give that person a business card of a shelter or whatever. So don't think this is that. He saw *you*. Being able to help you is just a bonus."

Summer had believed her.

They'd all made plans to keep in contact. Alabama, who was definitely the quietest of the bunch had bitched about the fact Summer didn't have a cell phone. She'd wanted to be able to text her and communicate with her that way. It made Summer feel good, but she stood her ground when they'd started talking about putting her on one of their family plans. It was one thing for Mozart to spend some money buying her some food. It was another to allow his *friends* to spend money on something so frivolous and unnecessary in her life.

So they'd agreed to communicate via the land-line phone that Summer had in her room. They'd promised to call when they got back to Riverton to let her know they'd arrived all right.

Summer pulled Fiona aside to thank her for her honest words the first night they'd been there. Fiona had blown it off, but Summer could tell it meant a lot to her.

Summer sighed heavily. She had the rooms to clean and another boring week ahead of her. It was amazing how uninteresting her life seemed now that she'd met both Mozart and his friends. Summer was nervous to meet the rest of his team, but the women had reassured her that they'd love her. Summer wasn't so sure, but it wasn't like she could do anything about it now. She was too practical. She had to get through this day first. Then the next. Then the next.

Summer was cleaning one of the rooms and day-dreaming about seeing Mozart again, when she heard a throat being cleared behind her. She jumped, knowing she needed to pay more attention when she was alone in the rooms. It'd be easy for someone to sneak up on her and close the door and assault her. She turned to see Joseph standing in the doorway.

"Jesus, Joseph, you scared me. What's up?"

"You should pay more attention to your surroundings, Summer," he told her with a weird look in his eyes.

"I know, I was just thinking that," Summer laughed nervously. Joseph had never made her nervous before, but he was certainly acting weird enough to make the hair on the back of her neck stand up. She couldn't help but remember how Fiona had thought Joseph was "creepy" as well. "Can I help you with something?"

"Yeah, I just wanted to tell you that I'm done with room two. It should be ready for guests again. Henry wanted me to tell you to go ahead and clean it and get it prepared."

"Okay, thanks for letting me know. I'll put it back on my rotation and get to it after I'm done with the other rooms." Summer watched as Joseph just stood there. "Was there anything else?"

"Are you seeing anyone?"

"What?"

"Are you seeing anyone?" he repeated in a flat tone of voice.

"Uh, actually I am." Summer wasn't going to apologize for it, but she wasn't sure what else to say. She hoped like hell Joseph wasn't going to ask her out. He was way too old for her, and she felt nothing toward him but a general kinship because they both worked at the motel.

"I haven't seen anyone around. Just those women who left today."

"Yeah, well, I am. Okay? He's in the military and

he's currently on a mission." As soon as the words left Summer's mouth she wished she could take them back. Why had she told Joseph Mozart wasn't around?

"I see. Well, it can't be too serious as I've only seen him once."

When he didn't say anything else, Summer stammered, "Well, it is."

"Hmm. Okay. Well, maybe you'll introduce me to your 'military man' the next time he's here."

"Yeah, sure. No problem, Joseph."

"Have a good day, Summer."

"You too." Summer let out a relieved sigh when Joseph left the doorway and headed toward the office, most likely to tell Henry he was done with whatever task he'd been assigned.

Summer cleaned the rest of the rooms with one eye constantly on the door to the room. She'd even closed the door all the way when she had to clean the bathrooms. She felt vulnerable after her weird conversation with Joseph, and didn't want anyone surprising her again.

Summer went to her room as soon as she was done for the day and closed and locked her door. She put on the chain as well as flipping the deadbolt. She shivered a bit, even though she wasn't really cold. The day had been weird, and it was all because of Joseph. She hadn't really even talked to the man before. She'd been introduced to him by Henry when he'd been hired, but after that they'd only exchanged waves and the typical "hi's" and "hellos" in passing.

For him to suddenly want to have a conversation about who she was dating was odd. She thought back to earlier that weekend. Alabama had seen him watching them and thought he was weird. *Was* he weird? Summer didn't know.

She made herself a salad and nuked a microwave meal for dinner. Knowing she needed to put some weight on she forced herself to eat a candy bar for dessert. Normally she relished the chocolate treat, not having been able to splurge on something as little as a candy bar in so long, but tonight it wasn't cutting it. She desperately wanted to talk to Mozart. To see him. To have him hold her and tell her it'd be fine. Summer leaned over and picked up the phone.

Hey, Mozart. It's me. For some reason it's not weird anymore for me to call you every day and leave you a message. It makes me feel closer to you. I find myself thinking of stuff I want to tell you during the day and I can't wait to pick up the phone and tell you. I'm looking forward to when you can actually talk back to me when I tell you about my day. The girls left today. I was sad to see them go. You were right. It's nice to talk to someone who understands about you being gone. They're going through the same thing as I am and it's good to be able to talk to them. They said they'd keep in touch. So thank you for that. I should've trusted you to know what you were talking about...and no you can't throw that back in my face when you get back. Something weird happened today with Joseph. I don't think I can really explain it over the phone though. It's probably nothing, but it was just out of the ordinary. He asked me if I was dating anyone. Which is weird because we haven't really talked before. Don't get upset, of course I told him I was. He backed off after that. Anyway, other than that, things are the same here. I ate the last candy bar you bought me today. I'll have to see about getting more of those, you got me addicted to them. I miss you, Mozart. I hope you're okay. I can't wait until you get back. Bye.

Summer put the phone back on its cradle on the little table and snuggled down into the covers on the bed. Her mind raced with all the things she wanted to say to Mozart. He hadn't even been gone a week yet, but she hoped like hell this mission would be one of the shorter ones. She'd feel better if he was back in California instead of who-knew-where. It wouldn't change their circumstances, she was here and he was in Riverton, but at least he'd be in the country and she could talk to him.

Chapter Thirteen

S UMMER GROANED WHEN the phone rang the next morning. She rolled over and saw it was only six thirty. She didn't even think about ignoring it though, because the only people that would be calling her were Mozart or his, and now her, friends.

"Hello?" Summer tried to sound more awake than she was. She had no idea why people did that, pretended to be awake when they weren't, but it seemed the polite thing to do.

"Sorry I woke you up, Summer. How are you?"

"Uh…who is this?" Summer knew it wasn't Mozart, she'd recognize his voice in an instant. She'd never heard this person before.

Chuckling, the person on the other end of the line said, "Sorry. I'm Tex. I think Mozart told you about me?"

"Yeah. What's wrong? Is Mozart okay?"

"Shit. Yeah. He's fine. Sorry, didn't mean to startle you. I just wanted to call and introduce myself. I know he told you to call me if you needed anything, but if you're anything like most women I know, you won't do it because you don't know me. So I'm calling so you can *get* to know me and you'll call if you need to."

Not knowing exactly why he was calling and not being all the way awake yet, Summer said, "Okay."

Tex chuckled on the other end of the phone. "First, you have to know what it is I do. If it has to do with something electronic, I can get information out of it. Phones, cameras, computers, credit card machines...anything."

"Are you a hacker?"

"Yes."

Whispering now, Summer said, "Is that legal?"

"I don't go around hacking into the FBI database for fun, Summer, if that's what you're asking. But if I need to find someone, or if one of my teams needs something, they'll find they have it."

"I don't understand how that's not illegal." Summer sat up in the bed, a little more awake now, and leaned against the headboard. She really wanted to understand this man. She heard the respect in Mozart's voice when he told her about Tex. She knew Mozart was an honest-to-God-hero, and he wouldn't champion someone who wasn't on the up-and-up.

"Let me give you an example. I hope you don't mind, but Mozart told me a bit about your situation. If you called me, as you're supposed to, if you run out of money for food and are hungry, all it takes is a few clicks and I can have the local grocery store deliver a week's worth of whatever it is that you want to eat, in about five minutes."

"But, that's stealing!" Summer, honestly shocked, informed him unnecessarily.

"I didn't say it wouldn't be paid for," Tex scolded.

Blushing, Summer muttered, "Oh."

"Yeah, Oh. I can arrange for food to be delivered to you remotely. I'd charge it to my credit card, or Mozart's, but it would be paid for. The point I'm trying to make here, sweetheart, is that you aren't alone out there. I can get whatever you need to do you remotely. I don't have to cheat or break the law in order to do it."

Summer let out a relieved breath.

Tex heard it and continued, "But, that isn't to say that I *wouldn't* do something illegal to help you if I needed to."

"You don't even know me though," Summer argued.

"I don't have to. You belong to Mozart. That's good enough for me."

Summer didn't have anything to say about that. On one hand she was appalled that Tex had actually said it out loud. It sounded so barbaric. But the other part of her, the part that had really listened to what Caroline,

Alabama, and Fiona had told her about the men, rejoiced in being a part of their close-knit family. The thought of "belonging" to Mozart also made her feel warm and fuzzy inside. It was official, she was insane.

"Well, I'm good. I don't need anything, legal or illegal."

"You'll call me if you do?" When she didn't say anything, Tex warned, "Summer?"

"Oh all right. Jeez. You're just like Mozart."

"Thank you."

"It wasn't a compliment," Summer said petulantly, even though she was smiling.

"I know. And Summer, the next time you go out drinking with the ladies, try the Madori Sours, they're just as good as the Amaretto Sours."

"Wha-, how do you know what I was drinking?"

"There are security cameras everywhere, Summer."

Summer was just cluing into how serious Tex was about what he did. "Okay. I'll try them then. Next time." She could hear Tex laughing at her.

"Good. Now go back to sleep. You have another couple of hours before you need to be up and cleaning. *Call me,* Summer. For anything you need. I'm here when Mozart can't be."

"Okay, Tex. Thank you."

"You're welcome. Have a good day."

"You too. Bye."

"Bye."

Hanging up the phone, Summer could only shake her head. Mozart's world was one she never expected to find herself in, but she couldn't deny that she liked it. She liked how protective he and his friends were. They were bossy and liked ordering people around, but she could tell that deep down they were very caring men. And she figured women like Caroline, Alabama, and Fiona wouldn't be with them, if they were assholes. That had to mean something.

She snuggled back down into the covers and closed her eyes. She'd do what Tex ordered just because *she* wanted to, not because he told her to.

"HEY, SUMMER, CAN you come here for a second?"

Summer turned and saw Henry standing at the door to the office gesturing for her to come over to him. She wiped her hands on the towel she'd been holding and draped it over the cart. She moved the cart as much to the side as she could, out of the way of any guests that might walk by, and set the brake on it. The last thing she wanted was it rolling away and dumping all the stuff on the ground. Summer hurried across the parking lot to the office.

She entered to see Joseph leaning against the front desk with Henry standing behind it. Summer immediately tensed. Ever since the weird encounter she had with Joseph a few days ago, she'd been edgy and nervous around him. They hadn't spoken since then, but she'd caught him looking at her a few times.

"What's up, Henry?" Summer said as normally as she could.

"I've been talking with Joseph and he's got an idea and we could use your help."

"Okay, I'll do what I can."

Joseph took over the conversation. "I told Henry we could probably get more women to stay here if we spruced up the rooms a bit more. Women, after all, are the ones who most often make room reservations for family vacations. I think if we changed out the paintings on the walls and upgraded the bedding, it would go a long way toward helping raise business."

Summer looked at Joseph closely. The words coming out of his mouth seemed so incongruent to his looks. He was probably around sixty-five years old and had long, stringy, gray hair. He wasn't skinny and he wasn't fat. He was actually in pretty good shape for an older guy. But there was something about him, now that Summer was paying attention, that just wasn't right. Joseph talking about bedding and pictures just didn't go with what she thought a handy man would even care about.

She cautiously answered. "Okay, yeah, that sounds

good. Was that what you wanted? For my approval and opinion?"

"Actually we need you for more," Henry told her. "I need for you to go with Joseph to town and pick out some things. We have no idea what women like, since you're female, you do. You guys can go this afternoon and get some stuff for a few of the rooms and we'll set them up and take pictures for the website tomorrow."

Summer stood stock still. Henry had never asked her to do anything like this before. She had no idea why he was suddenly interested in her opinion as a woman. Trying to get out of it she said, "Uh, I haven't finished cleaning the rooms yet."

"No problem. We don't have anyone renting them tonight, so they'll keep until tomorrow."

Shit. There went that excuse. Joseph hadn't said anything further, he was just standing next to the counter with his legs crossed at the ankle and smiling at her. Actually it looked more like a smirk. Summer had no idea what to say to get out of this, she'd never been any good at thinking on her feet. She usually came up with a good comeback about two days after the fact.

"Uh, okay."

"Great, here are the keys to my car. Joseph, go pull it around. Summer, meet Joseph out front."

"I have to make a phone call first," Summer blurted out. She couldn't get Tex's words out of her head. He'd keep an eye on her. If he could see what she'd been drinking when she'd been out with the other SEAL's women, maybe he could keep his eye on her while she was shopping with Joseph. Summer had no idea if that was even possible or not, but Tex *had* ordered her to call him if she needed anything.

"Okay, but make it quick. Time's a wastin'." Henry was feeling good about his decision to redecorate, and obviously wanted it done right away.

Summer pushed open the office door and made a beeline for her room. She pulled the keycard out of her back pocket and after entering, locked the door behind her. She went right to the phone and pulled the piece of paper with the phone numbers Mozart had left for her to the end of the table so she could read it. She'd kept it under the phone for easy reference.

She dialed Tex's phone number and listened to it ring. When it went to voicemail, Summer swore under her breath. Shit. He had to be there. She hung up and dialed the number again. When it again went to voice mail again, Summer sighed. She didn't have a choice but to leave a message.

Hey, Tex, it's Summer. I don't really know why I'm calling, except I needed some advice…or something. I've been asked to go into town with the guy Henry hired as a handy man for the motel. His name is Joseph. Normally I wouldn't think twice about it, but he's been...weird lately. Nothing bad, and I'm sure it's nothing, but since I don't have a car or anything I have to go with him. I thought that you could, maybe...shit. I don't know. Watch? You said there were cameras and you knew what I was drinking that one night....oh Jesus. I sound crazy. Anyway, okay, well, I have to go, he's waiting for me. I'll call you when I get back later and you can laugh at how paranoid I am. Bye.

Summer hung up the phone, took a deep breath, and walked to the door. She closed it carefully behind her, making sure it latched shut and saw Joseph waiting for her in Henry's old car. She smiled at Joseph nervously as she opened the door and closed it behind her. She looked behind her as they pulled out of the parking lot. *Big Bear Lake Cabins Motel* might be run-down and sad, but it held a special place in her heart because it was where she met Mozart. She'd do what she could to make it a success.

Chapter Fourteen

TEX CAME BACK into his apartment after taking a short walk. He was so close to finding Ben Hurst he could taste it. He'd just needed a small break before hitting the computer again. He wanted to find the asshole for Mozart, and to get him off the streets. The man was a menace and had been extremely lucky over his lifetime. He'd apparently made a habit out of assaulting women and children. Avery Reed wasn't his first victim, and certainly wasn't his last. There was something obviously wrong inside the man's head. He had no remorse for what he'd done and what he continued to do. Hurst's short stints in jail had no effect on his behavior.

Tex had traced the man to the Big Bear Lake area a few months ago and that's why Mozart had ended up there. Tex smiled. He loved being able to have one up on a fellow SEAL. He could now claim for the rest of their lives that he was the one who basically introduced Mozart to Summer.

Tex settled into his chair and wiggled his mouse. His computer screen lit up and he was happy to see his chat box blinking at him. He eagerly clicked on it and saw the note from Mel. Smiling at her comment, he quickly responded. He loved talking to her. She was smart and funny. It was weird because he had no idea what she looked like or even where she was, but she entertained him and gave him a good break from everything else he had going on in his life.

Thirty minutes later, he signed off with Mel reluctantly. He had work to do. He wanted to nail Hurst and needed to find where the bastard was hiding. Tex clicked on the icon to open a new browser and out of the corner of his eye saw the red light blinking on his cell phone. When did he miss a call? He remembered suddenly that he hadn't taken the phone when he'd left earlier for his walk.

He listened to the message from Summer and heard what she didn't say. It was obvious she was feeling uneasy about the situation, but she had no idea how to get out of it. If she hadn't been uneasy, she never would have called him. Shit. If Tex had been able to talk to her, he would've told her in no uncertain terms not to get in the car with Joseph. He'd learned to listen to his gut, more times than not, it was right.

Tex looked at the time of the message. It'd been over half an hour since Summer had called him. Fuck.

With purpose, Tex turned to his laptop and quickly brought up the security cameras he'd used to track Summer and the other women when they'd gone out. He rewound the footage about twenty-five minutes and combed through them all anxiously. He didn't see Summer in any of them.

Dammit. He quickly checked the other cameras that he was able to hack into, with no luck. Summer and the mysterious Joseph hadn't made it into town.

He checked the local law enforcement scanners. There had been no traffic accidents in the last half hour. He had no idea where Summer disappeared to, but he had a feeling the mysterious Joseph would turn out to be the man he'd spent the last few years tracking. Tex didn't know how he knew it, but with every minute that passed without sight of Summer, he knew he was right. Ben Hurst was at it again, and Tex had no idea how Mozart was going to react to the fact that the man who killed his little sister all those years ago, had now taken his woman.

SUMMER BLINKED SLOWLY. Fuck. She knew immediately she was in deep trouble. Just as they'd pulled around the corner from the motel, Joseph had hit her in the face hard enough to stun her. Her head had bounced off the side window and she saw stars. When Summer could finally think straight again, to try to open the door to get out, Joseph had already immobilized her. He'd pulled over on a side road and put a pair of handcuffs around her wrists behind her back, stuffed a piece of cloth in her mouth, and tied a gag around her head. Summer couldn't move and she couldn't talk. When she'd turned sideways and kicked Joseph as hard as she could in his ribs, he'd hit her again, this time hard enough to knock her out.

Now, here she was. Summer had no idea *where* she was, but she knew she wasn't safe. She choked back a sob. With the gag still in her mouth, she couldn't cry now. She was having a hard enough time breathing as it was. Why didn't she follow her instincts? She'd called Tex because she *knew* Joseph wasn't safe, but she didn't have the guts to say no. She moaned. Would she ever see Mozart again? Would she ever see *anyone* again?

TEX FRANTICALLY HIT the keys on his computer. Shit. Shit. Shit. He had to get Mozart and the rest of his team home. Tex shook his head. He spent too much of his damn life trying to get those SEALs back to the States when they were on a mission. It was uncanny how unlucky their women were. But there was no doubt in Tex's mind now that Hurst was Joseph. He'd called Henry at the motel and asked as many questions as he could about the handyman he'd hired.

Henry didn't know much about the man. He didn't know where he lived or even what his last name was. Henry had needed someone to do some grunt work around the motel, and Joseph had been his only applicant. Henry paid him in cash and had been happy with the work he'd been doing.

Tex hung up in disgust. Shit. Now what? He needed boots on the ground. This seemed to be one time when working from Virginia on the computer just wasn't going to cut it. He had to get Mozart home. Now.

"I'VE BEEN WAITING for you, Summer."

Summer glared at Joseph from across the room. She was in some sort of cabin, and it could have been anywhere in the mountains around the lake. She tried not to think about it, but instead, turned her mind to trying to figure out how the hell she was going to get out of the situation.

"I don't even know you, Joseph. Why would you be waiting for me?" Summer tried to keep her voice even, but she could hear the tremble in her voice. Joseph had taken the gag out of her mouth and even fed her a bit of food and given her some water. Summer had been reluctant to eat it at first, but after Joseph had eaten some of it to show it wasn't drugged, she'd given in. She knew she'd need her strength if she was going to get out of there.

"You have no idea who I am do you?"

"You're Joseph."

He laughed evilly. "I see your boyfriend hasn't really told you anything has he? You haven't spent time talking, I wonder what you've spent your time together doing?" Joseph sneered at Summer.

Summer didn't say anything, waiting for Joseph to get on with whatever it was he obviously wanted her to know.

"My name is Benjamin Hurst." When Summer didn't react in any way, he elaborated. "I kidnapped, raped, and killed Avery Reed years and years ago. In case *that* name doesn't ring any bells, I'll clue you in. I'm the man your boyfriend has been hunting since he was a teenager. I find it ironic he came up here to find me, and instead led me straight to your door. If he hadn't come back, I would've earned a bit of money working for Henry and slunk out of town as soon as the snow melted. Instead, I saw him with you. I couldn't resist."

"You killed his sister?"

"Oh yeah. But not before I raped and tortured her. There's nothing like the screams of a child, but alas, there aren't too many kids up here, so you'll have to do. And for the record, you *will* scream, Summer. I plan on raping and torturing you too, before I kill you. I've come a long way since little Avery. I know just how far to go before pulling back. I wouldn't want you to die before I'm ready."

Summer tried really hard to keep a straight face. Jesus. She couldn't think, she didn't know what to say. She kept her mouth shut and just watched as Joseph/Ben came toward her with the dreaded gag in his hand. She tried not to flinch, but couldn't help it. She was scared shitless.

"But first I need to go out. I can't risk you screaming so loudly that someone hears you, can I? Not that anyone would. We're so far out in the woods, it'd take a miracle for anyone to find you."

Before he could put the gag back in place, Summer spit out, "Mozart will find you and kill you. You might torture and end up killing me, but Mozart *will* find you. You'll wish you were dead when he does. You'll regret kidnapping me when the last thing you see is Mozart's face before he kills you."

Ben grabbed her jaw and squeezed so tightly, Summer couldn't help the whimper that escaped her lips. Her jaw opened involuntarily and Ben shoved the filthy piece of cloth back in her mouth. He quickly wrapped the piece of sheet around her head to keep the gag in place. When it was secured behind her, he leaned in and whispered, "I can't wait to see him, to show him what's left of your battered and beaten body. To watch him break down. I know he's a killer just like me. I want to see him lose it and kill out of anger. He's just like me, he just needs to be shown the way. Shown how cathartic it can be to take another's life."

Summer shivered. This man was crazy. She dropped her head. There would be no reasoning with him. She was as good as dead.

Chapter Fifteen

M OZART CLUTCHED THE arms of the seat in the
military plane with all his strength. They'd been
getting ready to head home when Wolf had gotten a
message on their emergency satellite phone. The phone
was only used in extreme emergencies back home.
Mozart and the others had waited anxiously to hear
what the issue was. Abe and Cookie were hoping like
hell it wasn't anything to do with their women. Mozart
wasn't too worried for himself, Summer was up in Big
Bear working at the motel. But he was concerned for his
friends.

When Wolf had come back to them and said bluntly that Summer had disappeared, Mozart at first didn't
understand what he'd said.

"Did you hear me, Mozart?" Wolf had asked gently.

"What do you mean, disappeared? What was the
message?" All Mozart could think was that maybe she'd
decided she didn't want to be with him anymore and
had just left.

"Tex got a hold of the Commander. Summer called Tex. The handyman at the hotel where she was working is Hurst. He's got her, Mozart." Wolf didn't beat around the bush.

Before he could jump Wolf and beat the crap out of him for lying, Dude and Cookie grabbed his arms. "No! Not Summer! It can't be true! Tell me it's not true!"

"I'm sorry, Mozart. We're heading home now. He won't fucking get away with this."

Mozart clenched his teeth. Joseph was Hurst? Had he known Summer was his? Had he seen him around the motel? Had Hurst targeted Summer because of him? Deep down Mozart knew the truth. He had. He'd been the reason Summer was taken. He'd get her back. No matter what it took. Somehow he knew Hurst was waiting for him to get there. He wanted to confront him. He wanted to throw Avery in his face. Mozart was ready. Summer was all that mattered.

SUMMER SAT STOCK still and watched as Ben carried someone into the little cabin over his shoulder. He dropped the slight woman as if she was nothing more than a sack of potatoes. The sound her body made as it thunked to the floor, made her wince.

Ben turned toward Summer. "Look what I found!" He sounded gleeful. "Another toy! I think I'll play with this one first before I start with you. I want you to see and know what's in store for you. I want you to think about it. To see it happening to someone else first." Ben squatted down in front of Summer. "Everything I do to her, I'll do to you. Every scream she makes, know you'll make as well. The anticipation is the best part."

Summer shuddered. She didn't recognize the woman lying unconscious on the floor, but she could see blood oozing out around a wound on the side of her temple. Summer shut her eyes, not wanting to see.

A blow to the side of her head brought her eyes open in a flash. "Keep your eyes open, bitch," Ben hissed. "If you close them, I'll make it hurt worse for her. Remember that." Summer nodded, knowing he'd do exactly what he said.

"I'll wait until she comes to, then we'll begin."

Summer allowed one tear to fall before ruthlessly pushing them back. This man wouldn't get any more of her tears. He'd enjoy them too much. She just had to hold on. She'd called Tex. Mozart would come. He had to.

As SOON AS they landed, Mozart turned his phone on. He needed to see if Summer had called him. Maybe it was all a misunderstanding. He had eight messages. He listened to them one right after another. Tears came to his eyes. The last time he'd cried was at Avery's funeral, but listening to Summer blithely talking about how her day went and saying she missed him at the end of every message made him die a bit inside.

What if your message space gets used up and some-one important needs to leave you a message?

Jesus. Didn't Summer know that *she* was someone important? That there was no one he'd rather hear from, than her?

Joseph has been working on upgrading the rooms a bit... He's been a great help around here.

It tore Mozart's heart in two to hear Summer talking so nicely about Hurst, and having no idea who he was, *what* he was.

I like them. I like your friends. I'm so glad you have friends that will look out for you. And just so you know, I like you. I can handle what you do. I can handle your job. If you really want to be with me. I'm here.

Hearing her talk about liking Fiona, Alabama, and Caroline made Mozart feel good. He knew Summer would like them. Hearing her say she liked *him* and that she could handle what he did would've made him feel on top of the world, if she wasn't currently in the hands of a madman.

Fiona thought Joseph was creepy but I tried to tell her he wasn't, he's just a loner, like I was. But I'm not anymore. I have you.

Alabama could tell he wasn't trustworthy. She knew. Why the hell didn't Summer see it?

Something weird happened today with Joseph. He asked me if I was dating anyone.

Mozart closed his eyes. Hurst knew. He *knew* Summer was his. Mozart had known it in his gut, but hearing Summer validate it, tore his heart in two. He clenched his fists. He had to get there in time. He had to. Mozart saved all of Summer's messages to listen to again later. He wanted to listen to them again when Summer was safe in his arms. He wanted to treasure them. A little voice inside his head tried to say that the reason he was keeping them was because if Summer died, he wanted to keep a piece of her, but he refused to listen. They'd get there in time. Hurst wanted him there. Mozart was convinced. Hurst wouldn't kill Summer until he'd arrived in Big Bear.

SUMMER KEPT HER eyes open while Ben tortured the poor woman on the floor in front of her. She was gagged, like Summer. He'd tied her hands together and attached them to a stake in the floor of the cabin. Her ankles were tied together with a piece of rope and then connected to a hook in the wall across the room. She was rendered helpless, stretched out on the hard cold floor, vulnerable and open for anything Ben wanted to do to her. To add insult to injury, Ben had also cut all of her clothes off so the poor woman lay naked on the floor whimpering. Ben had started his torture out by holding his hand over her mouth and nose while at the same time choking her with the other.

Ben laughed as she started turning blue, but let up on her neck and face at the last minute, letting her inhale precious oxygen to keep her conscious. In between choking her, he'd slap and hit her. Summer could see bruises all over the woman's body from the beatings she'd been given. The entire time Ben tortured the poor woman, he was looking at Summer.

"Watch, sweet Summer. See what I'm doing. See how she gasps for breath? This'll be you. I'll make you bleed just like she is. Your skin will bruise up even better than hers does. You'll have my marks all over you. At first you'll beg me to let you live, just like she's done. Eventually, you'll be begging me to kill you. You'll die all right. Just like she will. Slowly and painfully. Just how I like it."

Ben looked down at the woman beneath him for the first time. He leaned toward her and whispered in her ear. Summer couldn't hear what he said, but she saw the woman shake her head and mouth the word "no." Hurst just laughed and got up off her limp body on the floor. Whatever he'd said seemed to leave the woman broken and no longer willing to fight.

Ben didn't even look at the woman bleeding and gasping for breath. He came to Summer and leaned into her. His hands were covered in the woman's blood and he had a crazed look in his eye. He came way too close her for Summer's comfort. Ben took her face in his hands, smearing the woman's blood on her cheeks. He leaned in, and Summer could smell him. His body odor was atrocious. He'd been sweating and obviously hadn't showered in days, at least. He licked up the side of Summer's neck, laughing when she shook and strained against her bonds.

He brought his lips to Summer's ear, whispering intimately, as if they were lovers, "I told her you enjoyed watching. That you got off on it. I told her *you* were the one who wanted me to hurt her."

Summer glared at Ben. She was appalled at his words; the mental torture he was putting the other woman through was just as brutal as the physical abuse. She tried not to react in any other way to what he said though. Summer knew that was what Ben wanted, and she'd resist him with everything she could.

Ben was obviously pissed at Summer's lack of reaction. He undid his pants and pulled out his wrinkled and soft penis and proceeded to stroke himself until he was semi-hard. Summer looked away, repulsed. As Ben ran his hand up and down his manhood, he whispered about what he was going to do with Summer when it was her turn. When he'd gotten himself close to completion, his head went back and he groaned. Ben aimed his release at Summer and it splattered onto her. His cum landed in her lap and oozed down her restrained legs.

Ben's head came up and he laughed at the look of disgust on Summer's face. He brought his hand down to her lap and for a second Summer was confused, thinking he meant to clean it off of her, but then Ben palmed her cheek roughly in the hand he'd just run over his release in her lap. Ben smeared his semen on Summer's face and even ran his hand over her hair. The smell and feel of the wetness made her gag. Ben brought his hand back down to her face and squeezed Summer's cheeks until she couldn't help but grimace in pain. "Oh, Summer. When will you learn that I always fucking win?"

Ben turned and walked away, ignoring the pitiful whimpers from the bound and gagged woman on the cold floor. Summer waited until he left the room before closing her eyes and letting despair wash over her.

MOZART STOOD IN the room at the base with his back to his friends listening as Tex's voice came from the speaker phone and told them everything he'd learned over the last day and a half. He clenched his teeth in frustration and fury. He wanted to be up at Big Bear Lake looking for Summer. He *needed* to be up there. But they had to wait to hear what Tex had found out. They needed his information.

"Apparently Hurst has been staying in the woods in various places in the summers. In the winter he finds small towns to stay in. He works as a handy man here and there earning the odd dollar. Every place I've tracked him I've found dead bodies in his wake. Children, teenagers, old women, it doesn't matter. Other than being female, he doesn't seem to have a type. But every single one of the bodies had been tortured and raped."

"*People.*" Mozart growled suddenly from his spot against the wall. "Every single one of the *people* had been tortured and raped." He hadn't turned around and hadn't even spoken that loudly. Everyone in the room heard him though.

"Sorry, Mozart. Yes. All of the people that were found had been tortured before they were killed. It seems as if he chose Big Bear Lake for this winter to hole up. We were right, he was there, and it looks like he did know about you. He showed no interest in Summer until you left that second time. He targeted her."

Ignoring the pain coursing through his body at Tex's words, Mozart said, "Where did he take her?"

"I don't know."

Losing his cool for the first time since he'd heard the news that his Summer had been taken, Mozart turned around and yelled, "Where the hell is she, dammit? He's fucking torturing her. I know it. She needs me and I'm not there! I'm. Not. *There!*"

"We'll find her, Mozart," Wolf said in a low voice.

"When? After he's raped her over and over and gouged out her eyes? After she's nothing but a shell of the woman I left? When, Wolf? *When* will we find her? I thought Tex could find anybody!"

"I can, Mozart, when they're using modern technology," Tex responded calmly, his voice sounding eerie coming from the little speaker on the phone. "Hurst isn't using *any* technology. He's completely off the grid. No phones, no electric bills, no credit cards. He's living somewhere in the woods. Wherever he has your woman, it's in the middle of nowhere. It's too cold to have her tied to some tree, but it has to be a cabin or something."

"We need to get up there, Wolf," Mozart said hoarsely to his friend, not caring how he sounded. "Summer needs me. Now. Not in an hour, not tomorrow. Now."

"The helicopter's getting prepped as we speak, Mozart. We're going as soon as it's ready."

Mozart nodded.

The room was quiet for a moment, then Tex started talking excitedly. "Holy shit. Hang on. I'm getting a report from the cops up there about another missing woman. Elizabeth Parkins, twenty-two years old. Someone saw her being snatched right outside the local Walmart. Hold on....yeah, okay, I've got the surveillance video that was given to the police. Oh yeah, that's fucking Hurst all right. Let me just check something..."

Every man in the room held their breath. They could hear the clacking of the computer keys as Tex frantically typed on his keyboard.

"Yes! Okay, Elizabeth had her cell phone with her and it was on until about three hours ago. Cell phone towers pinged it as it traveled along State Road 38 and then up Polique Canyon Road toward Bertha Peak. Signal was lost about eight miles up the road. He has to be taking Elizabeth to his hideout. And if he has Elizabeth, there's a good chance that's where you'll find Summer."

Tex's excitement didn't carry to the rest of the SEALs standing in the room. They all knew if Hurst had taken another woman so soon after kidnapping Summer, he'd either already killed Summer, or he had something else horrible planned.

"Helicopter's here," Benny said quietly into the

sudden silence in the room.

"Tex, stay in touch, let me know whatever information you get as soon as you get it," Wolf ordered as the team began to head out of the room to the waiting helicopter. Mozart was leading the way, they all knew if it would've sped up the timetable for leaving, he would've been running.

"Save her, Wolf," Tex said softly, obviously having waited until he could hear the others leave the room.

"We plan on it, Tex," Wolf returned, just as softly. He clicked off the phone and followed his team out the door. They had one of their own to find and rescue.

Chapter Sixteen

SUMMER COULDN'T HOLD back her tears anymore. She'd been brave for as long as she could, now she was scared shitless. She grunted and twisted against the handcuffs. They were already tight, but as she struggled, they dug in even more. Blood oozed down her hands to drip on the floor below her, but Summer didn't even feel the pain anymore. Watching Ben hurt the woman in front of her, had finally broken her.

"Mumph, Peas stmp. *Peas.*" The gag in her mouth prevented Summer from articulating what it was she wanted to say, but it was obvious Ben understood her mumbled words.

He laughed and held the lit cigarette once more to the poor woman's chest. She'd passed out about ten minutes ago, but Ben hadn't stopped. He continued to burn her flesh, pausing only to relight and puff on the cigarette each time it was snuffed out on the hapless woman's skin. Ben looked Summer in the eyes while he continued to hurt the woman lying motionless on the ground.

"Yeah, that's what I like to see. *Beg* me to stop, bitch."

Summer looked on in horror. He'd grown hard while torturing the poor woman. He was getting off on what he was doing. Even knowing she was playing right into his hands and doing exactly what he'd manipulated her into doing, Summer couldn't stop her whimpering behind the gag wrapped tightly around her face.

"Remember, this is gonna be you. Everything I'm doing to her, I'll do to you too. You want me to stop? You want me to wait until she's conscious again? I will if you want me to."

Summer shook her head frantically. Jesus no. Where was Mozart? She needed him more than she'd ever needed anyone in her entire life before.

"ARE YOU SURE you're under control?" Wolf asked, eying Mozart intently.

Mozart simply nodded once.

"Because if you're not, you'll put her in even more danger."

Mozart nodded sharply again, but still didn't say a word.

Wolf just looked at Mozart for a second, then turned to the rest of the group. They'd spent the last thirty minutes scoping out the lay of the land. Hurst's cabin was sitting in a small clearing about two miles from the nearest gravel road. There was a four-wheeler parked in front of the door, obviously Hurst's transportation to and from the road. They hadn't found a car yet, but they hadn't looked for it. They were all focused on getting to Summer and Elizabeth.

The cabin was a piece of shit. It was small, only about two hundred or so square feet and it had two small windows, one in the back and one on the side. There was a sad looking front porch listing to one side.

Mozart clenched his hands at his sides. Standing there, listening to Wolf outline the plan one last time to the team was literally killing him. His heart was beating too fast and he could feel his breaths coming way too shallowly.

He was trained for this type of thing. They all were, but it was a completely different thing when it was someone you loved who was in danger. Mozart paused for a moment, letting his thoughts sink in. Yes. He loved Summer. It was quick, yeah, but it felt right. The feeling settled into Mozart's gut and didn't make him panic or feel trapped. He now knew how Wolf had felt when Ice had been kidnapped. This was the worst feeling in the world. He knew he should be taking deep breaths to calm his heart rate and ready himself for what was to come, but it was physically impossible.

Wolf, seemingly able to read his mind, turned to him. "Mozart, talk to me. Where are you at here?"

Liking the fact that Wolf wasn't ordering him around, but trusting him to know where he might be the most useful, Mozart answered tersely. "You take lead. I'll go in behind you." Wolf had been there. He'd let his team members take the front line to rescue Ice, and they'd delivered her back into his arms safe and sound. If Wolf had been able to do it, so could he.

Wolf put one hand on Mozart's shoulder briefly, before nodding and turning to the others.

"Okay, Dude, you take the side window and deploy the flashbang. After it's gone off, Cookie will make entry through the back window and Benny will go in through the side. Mozart and I will take the front door. Dude, you and Abe stand outside just in case Hurst decides to make a run for it. Our first objective here is to protect the women. Whatever it takes. Got it?"

All the men nodded solemnly. They knew what Wolf wasn't saying. They were ready.

"You all know it'll be crazy in there for a moment. That cabin isn't big enough to hold all of us comfortably, so be sure about your movements." Wolf paused for a beat then said, "Whatever you see in there, don't lose your heads."

"Fuck," Mozart said under his breath, knowing exactly what Wolf meant. He couldn't even think of

Summer not being all right. He knew he should feel bad about the other woman as well, but his mind was filled with thoughts of Summer. He saw how she'd tried to be polite when she was literally starving and trying not to show it. He remembered how they'd laughed together while they'd cleaned the damn hotel rooms. Mozart even remembered how she'd felt in his arms. He had no idea what condition they'd find her in, and that sliced through him more than anything.

"Mozart, you have to keep your cool with Hurst. If he's alive when the dust settles, you can't go all vigilante on us. You hear me?"

Mozart jolted and his eyes careened with his buddy's. "Jesus, Wolf," he whispered dumbfounded, "I hadn't even thought about Hurst. All I can think about is Summer."

"Good," Wolf returned immediately. "I wasn't sure. You trust us right?"

"Yes, with my fucking life and with Summer's," Mozart said without hesitation.

"We'll take care of Hurst. He won't hurt anyone else after today. You have my word on that."

Mozart looked around. Every man was looking at him with determination and intent in their eyes. He relaxed. For the first time in his life something, no someone, was more important than his vendetta against Ben Hurst. He threw a silent prayer up to Avery, asking for her forgiveness in putting Summer first.

As if able to read his mind, Abe said, "Avery would want you to move on. No matter what, she'd want you to move on."

Mozart nodded. His heart finally slowed and he got a handle on the adrenaline coursing through his body. Abe was right. Avery would've been pissed at him for putting his life on hold. She'd tell him that Hurst wasn't worth all the effort he'd put into him over the years. She would've loved Summer.

"Let's do this."

The men nodded and everyone but Wolf and Mozart faded away silently into the woods to get into position.

Needing to say one last thing before everything went down, Mozart turned to Wolf.

"Make him pay."

"I got this, Sam," Wolf said, using Mozart's real name for the first time in a long time. "You take care of your woman, we'll take care of Hurst."

Mozart looked his friend in the eye for a beat, then nodded. No more words were needed.

Both men turned toward the cabin and waited. The shit was about to hit the fan.

SUMMER'S EYES WERE open, but she wasn't seeing

anything. She'd turned her brain off to protect herself. Ben Hurst was evil. He'd been torturing the woman, whose name she finally learned was Elizabeth, for hours. Every time Summer had closed her eyes, Ben had hit her in order to force her to open her eyes again. When she wouldn't stop closing her eyes, Ben had taken two pieces of duct tape and taped Summer's eyelids open. She physically couldn't close her eyes anymore. Summer wouldn't give up though. Ben might have physically made it so her eyes had to remain open, but he couldn't force her to *see* what he was doing.

Ben had no idea that even though Summer's eyes were open, she was seeing Mozart. Instead of seeing the long knife wound Ben had carved into Elizabeth's side, she saw the looks on the faces of the bitches maligning Mozart the first time she'd met him. Summer remembered how she'd run her hands up and down his chest, reveling in the feel of Mozart's cut body and seeing the look of jealousy in the other women's faces at her words.

Instead of seeing Ben's hands cruelly squeezing Elizabeth's breasts until finger sized bruises formed, Summer saw the look on Mozart's face as he palmed her own breasts and erotically pinched her nipple. The look of pure rapture and lust on Mozart's face would be engrained in her brain forever. Summer never thought she could make a man feel or look like that. The fact she'd done it without even being undressed, was even more of a miracle.

Instead of hearing Ben's threats of her upcoming torture, she heard Mozart calling her "Sunshine." She laughed inside at his exasperated mutterings of, "you're a pain in my ass," and thought about how she couldn't wait to find other ways to make him laugh and smile at her.

Instead of hearing Ben rant about how her mutilated dead body would never be found after he buried her deep in the woods, Summer remembered how safe she'd felt in Mozart's arms and how he'd purposely taken the side of the bed next to the door, just so he could protect her.

And instead of feeling the slaps and hits from Ben as he tried to terrify her with his threats, Summer remembered the feel of Mozart's arms around her as he walked next to her, stood next to her, and slept next to her.

Suddenly the room erupted into chaos. Because her eyes were taped open, she couldn't protect herself from the blinding flash of light that suddenly filled the room. The quiet of the day, the slaps, moans, and crying she'd gotten too used to hearing, were drowned out by the loudest noise she'd ever heard. Summer wished she could bring her hands up to her ears to cover them, to protect them, but they were still securely cuffed behind her back.

She was completely blinded by the flash of light that

accompanied the loud bang and she felt physically nauseous from the loud noise. Summer shook her head, trying to get some of her senses back. She had no idea what was going on, but she wanted to stay in the place in her head where she'd felt safe in Mozart's arms.

Summer felt hands on her face, but still couldn't see who it was or what was going on. She tried to jerk out of way, but was held fast to the chair by the cuffs. She whimpered.

Finally a few words made their way through the ringing in her ears.

"…hold on…safe…fuck…help…"

Summer desperately tried to regain her faculties. She had to know what the hell was going on. Slowly she began to see shapes instead of the inky gray she'd been seeing since whatever had blown up had…well…blown up.

Her eyes hurt, were dry beyond belief, and Summer knew she'd been hoping Mozart would find her, but seeing his face in front of hers was a miracle she wasn't sure she could believe yet. She hoped she wasn't hallucinating. Summer jerked again, forgetting for a moment that her hands were still bound. She wanted to throw herself into his arms, but she couldn't.

"Thank fuck," Summer heard Mozart say. She watched as his face slowly came into more and more focus.

"Stay with me, Sunshine. I know you're in pain. I know the flashbang fucked with your senses, just give it a minute and it'll be safe for me to help you."

Summer didn't really understand anything Mozart was saying, she was too glad he was there. He'd keep her safe. He wouldn't let Ben hurt her. Suddenly she remembered Elizabeth. "Mpsbth."

Mozart answered as if she'd spoken perfectly understandable English, "Cookie has her. She's okay."

Summer didn't look away from Mozart's eyes. She could vaguely hear a commotion going on behind him, but at the moment she didn't care. All she cared about was that Mozart was there with her. He was actually there. He wouldn't let Ben touch her again. Summer breathed heavily through her nose.

"All clear!"

At the words, Mozart moved quickly. He bought a knife up from somewhere and Summer felt the gag that had been tied around her face loosen. She whimpered and tried to spit out the bunched up cloth from her mouth. Her mouth was way too dry to be able to rid herself of the nasty piece of fabric.

Mozart put the knife on the ground, and gently took Summer's chin in his. "Hold still, Sunshine. Let me help."

He reached between her dry cracked lips and grasped the edge of the material that was in her mouth.

Mozart didn't even bother to look at it as he flung it away once it cleared her lips. Mozart tried not to let the way she gasped for breath get to him. He couldn't. There were too many other things he had to do to help her first.

"I have to get the tape off your eyes, Sunshine," he whispered. "It's going to hurt. I'm sorry. I'm so sorry. It'll hurt for just a moment, then it will feel so good to be able to close your eyes. Okay? Do you understand?"

At her small nod, Mozart reached for the tape above her right eye. He had no idea if Hurst had known what he was doing, but he'd managed to get the tape on so that it was sticking to her eyelashes, eyebrows, and even some of her hair. Mozart hadn't lied. It was going to hurt coming off, but it couldn't wait for the hospital. Her eyes were bloodshot and dilated. She was in shock, and it had to be done.

Mozart wasn't sure if it would be better to rip it off, like a Band-Aid, but he decided to go slow and steady. When Summer didn't even moan as the tape ripped out the hair of her eyebrows and lashes, he knew her shock was worse than he'd thought. Seeing the little hairs on the tape as it came off, physically hurt him. Summer hadn't so much as whimpered throughout the ordeal though. As soon as the last piece of tape was off, Mozart watched as her eyes closed and she sighed.

Mozart stood up while saying, "Okay, Sunshine,

you're doing great. I'm going to get these cuffs off then we're out of here."

"Don't touch me."

Mozart took a step back as if Summer had physically hit him. He'd wanted to hear her speak to him, to reassure him that she was okay, but hadn't expected her first words to be for him to get away from her. "What?" The word came out before Mozart could pull it back.

"Don't touch me," Summer repeated.

Ignoring what was happening behind him, Mozart couldn't give a shit about Hurst at the moment. His focus was centered on Summer, and only Summer. Who the hell knew what Hurst had done to her while they were trying to find her. He'd only gotten a glimpse of the young woman who'd been strapped to the floor, but if Summer had been through anything like what it looked like the young woman had been though, it was no wonder she didn't want to be touched.

"Sunshine, I have to touch you to get the cuffs off."

Mozart watched as her eyes opened to slits. Her words tore through him.

"I'm not clean. He jacked off on me. He wiped her blood on me. He spit on me. He smeared his fucking cum on my face and hair. I don't want him anywhere on you."

Mozart's stomach turned. Fuck. He brought his hand to her face and put it over her eyes lightly. "Sunshine, keep your eyes closed, I know they hurt. I don't give a fuck what he did to you. I'm here now, I'll take care of you. *Let* me take care of you."

"I…Okay." Summer's voice was so soft, Mozart could barely hear it, but he *had* heard it. He brushed the knuckles of one hand down her cheek briefly before standing up again. He pulled a set of handcuff keys out of his pocket. Handcuffs keys were generally pretty standard and they were a part of the team's general supplies they carried with them at all times. They'd come in very handy in the past when they'd gotten into some sticky situations as well as when they'd gone in for a hostage rescue.

Mozart made quick work of unlocking the cuffs and winced at the condition of Summer's wrists. They were covered in blood and he could see deep gouges in her wrists from fighting against the cuffs' hold. Mozart dropped the metal handcuffs on the ground and took hold of Summer's hands with his. He walked around her careful not to jar her and kneeled in front of her again.

"I'm going to pick you up, Sunshine, and take you outside and away from here. I want you to hold on to me, don't let go, and keep your eyes closed. It's bright outside and I know the light will hurt your eyes."

He watched as Summer nodded, then she squeezed his hands.

"Is Elizabeth going to be all right?"

Mozart thought about lying to her, but decided she needed to hear the truth. "I don't know. I've only been concerned about you."

He leaned over and picked Summer up and settled her into his arms. She immediately rested her head on his shoulder and wound her arms around his neck.

"His name isn't Joseph."

"I know."

"It's Ben Hurst. He said he's been torturing and killing women and kids for years."

"Shhhh, I know, Summer."

"He said…"

"Sunshine," Mozart said a bit more forcefully as he maneuvered them to the door of the small cabin. "I *know*."

Mozart looked back into the room for the first time. Cookie had cut Elizabeth free and was trying to tend to her injuries. Benny and Dude were holding a subdued Hurst. His pants were around his ankles and his face was bloody. Wolf was standing over Hurst holding his pistol in his hand. Wolf met Mozart's eyes as he stopped at the door.

Mozart knew what Wolf wanted to know, but he didn't feel capable of making the decision. Once upon a time, he knew he would've wanted to be the one standing over Hurst, making him beg for his life, but he just didn't care anymore.

Even with holding an injured and traumatized Summer in his arms, he felt lighter. He felt as if he'd finally let go of all the angst and bitterness he'd held since he was fifteen over what Hurst had taken from him. In a weird way, Hurst had brought him and Summer together. If it hadn't been for Hurst hiding out in Big Bear, he never would've met Summer.

Mozart just wanted to get Summer out of the cabin and into some fresh air. He needed to get her to a hospital and he needed to make sure she was all right. Nothing else mattered. Not even Hurst.

Mozart turned away from Wolf and left the cabin. He heard Hurst yelling at him as he left the cabin, but Mozart didn't care. Whatever the man had to say, it didn't matter anymore.

Mozart saw that Abe was standing outside. He met his eyes and walked toward him.

"We need to get her to a hospital."

"I've got the four wheeler ready. It looks like its got lots of gas in it. You can't drive and hold Summer at the same time and three people won't fit on it. We also need to get help for Elizabeth. I'll head down to the car and get a hold of Tex. He'll get a chopper up here."

Mozart wasn't letting go of Summer. Not until he had to. "I'm not leaving her."

"Of course you aren't. Don't worry, Mozart. She's

made it this far, she'll be fine. I'll make sure Tex knows there'll be three people the chopper's picking up."

"Appreciate it." He turned to walk further away from the cabin and to get into the shade of some trees.

Abe turned to leave just as a single shot rang out from the cabin behind them. Abe stopped and turned around and looked at Mozart. Mozart hadn't veered from his path to the shade and in fact hadn't even turned around. Abe shook his head grimly, knowing what the shot meant. Hurst wouldn't be hurting anyone else ever again.

Finally, he shrugged, he had to get back to the cars and get a hold of Tex. Both women needed to get to a hospital immediately. They'd deal with Hurst and the aftermath of what had gone down later.

Chapter Seventeen

MOZART SAT NEXT to Summer's hospital bed with his feet propped up on the end of the mattress and watched her breathe. He watched as Summer's chest slowly moved up and down and he counted her breaths. She was breathing about sixteen times a minute, which was still in the normal range, but was toward the top of it.

She'd scared him to death, and Mozart wasn't afraid to admit it. Tex had worked fast and they'd been taken to the Community Hospital of San Bernardino, the closest trauma center to Big Bear. Within a couple of hours, Ice, Alabama, and Fiona had arrived, along with the rest of the team.

Mozart had stayed by Summer's side and had refused to leave. He'd told the doctor that Summer was his fiancée, and every member of his team had backed him up. Summer hadn't even contradicted him. He'd been allowed to stay while they'd examined her physically. Her clothes had been put into paper bags for the police as evidence, and a crime scene investigator had arrived to document her injuries with photographs.

Mozart stayed in the room, even when the nurses had tried to chase him out before they gave her a sponge bath to clean her up. He turned his back, so as not to embarrass Summer, but he wouldn't leave.

Summer hadn't said much during the exams, but Mozart noticed that she constantly checked to see where he was. Hardly a minute went by where she wasn't searching for him. Mozart made sure to stay within her eyesight. If the doctor moved so he blocked Summer's view of him, Mozart would step to the side, so she could still see him. Someone else might not have even noticed she was doing it, but he'd noticed and made sure she felt as comfortable as possible during the uncomfortable exam.

While the doctors checked her eyes, Mozart had held Summer's hand and didn't complain a bit when her fingernails dug into his skin. It wasn't until he saw the damage that had been done to her wrists that he'd broken down. Mozart hadn't been able to stop the tears that fell silently from his eyes. He'd seen worse injuries in his lifetime, but it was what the deep gouges meant, that made him lose it.

He knew Summer had fought. She'd fought against what Hurst had done to Elizabeth. She'd tried to escape. Mozart knew she'd continued to try to escape her bindings, even when it was obvious she couldn't. Even as the blood coursed down her hands and dripped on the floor below, she continued to fight.

Summer had seen his tears and leaned into him. She couldn't touch him since the nurses were cleaning and stitching her wrists, but she still found a way to comfort him. She turned her head and nuzzled into his neck as he cried. She sighed as Mozart's arms went around her tightly. Summer had simply whispered, "I'm okay, Mozart," and continued to let him take her weight until the nurses were done. They'd given her a shot for pain and the last thing she'd said to him was, "please don't leave."

So here he sat. She'd asked him not to leave and nothing was going to tear him away from her side. Not his commander, not the United States Navy, not the damn President of the United States. Mozart would sit there until hell froze over if he had to.

Each one of the girls had tiptoed into the room to see how Summer was doing. They hadn't known her very long, but she'd obviously made an impression on them. Summer had slept through all of their visits. The girls had promised to come back the next day when hopefully Summer would be awake.

Caroline had to get back to Riverton, she was in the middle of a huge project at work and really couldn't spare even one day away, but she'd insisted on coming up to visit anyway. It meant even more to Mozart because he knew first-hand how much Ice hated hospitals. Mozart had pulled her aside and asked for a favor. Of course, Caroline had agreed with no questions asked. Mozart smiled, remembering. Caroline probably would have been pissed if he *hadn't* asked for her help.

Ice had given him a big hug and told him, "She'll be okay, Mozart. She'll want you here. I'll see you guys back home."

Mozart thought back to when Ice had been in the hospital. She'd also been kidnapped and tortured. He hoped Summer would be able to get past everything that had been done to her as well as Ice had. He knew Ice still had some nightmares. He and Wolf had even talked about it. But slowly she was getting over them, thank God.

Summer finally stirred. Mozart brought his feet down and stood up. He sat down on the bed next to her hip and leaned over her, being careful not to jostle her. He didn't want to freak her out, but he wanted to be close enough so she'd know he was there the second she opened her eyes. With his hands on either side of her hips, Mozart surrounded her with his heat and leaned in, watching as Summer struggled to fully awaken.

Summer squirmed on the bed, not wanting to wake up. She knew if she opened her eyes, she'd have to deal with all the crap that had gone down over the last day or so. She remembered almost every second she'd been held in the cabin. As much as she wished she didn't, Summer knew she'd never forget. Every single part of her body hurt, but she was alive. She tried to keep telling herself that.

Summer opened her eyes to slits trying to keep her panic down. She knew it would be a long time before she'd feel comfortable being by herself again. Summer jolted at seeing a pair of intense dark eyes right above her head. She immediately relaxed. She'd recognize Mozart's eyes anywhere.

"Hi," she said quietly, relieved at seeing him there.

"Hey. How are you feeling?"

"You want the truth, or the watered down version?"

"Always the truth, Sunshine. Always."

"My wrists hurt. My eyes are burning, I feel dirty and I'm worried about Elizabeth. But I'm so relieved you're here I'm not sure I can put it into words. It makes all the other things fade away." Summer watched as Mozart's face at first tensed at her words, but then relaxed.

"There's no place I'd rather be."

"I called Tex like you told me to."

"Are we going to talk about this now? Or do you need time?"

"I'd rather talk about it now. I don't think I can ignore it for too long. It'll eat away at me."

"Do you want me to get a psychiatrist in here for you? I know Ice still talks to one and she's helped her a lot."

"No, I just want you."

"You've got me, Sunshine. Scoot over."

Mozart waited as Summer moved a bit to the right, then he lay down right next to her and gathered her into his arms carefully. He heard her sigh in contentment.

"Is this even legal?"

"Don't care."

Summer smiled at Mozart's words. She knew he really didn't care about the hospital rules. She sobered. "This is what I thought about when he made me watch. I wasn't seeing what he was doing or saying, I was remembering how safe I felt when you held me just like this."

"You did good calling Tex, but dammit, Summer, I have to say it. You shouldn't have gotten in the damn car with Hurst in the first place."

"I know."

Mozart paused. He was all ready to deliver a gentle, but firm reprimand, and Summer took all the wind out of his sails.

She continued, "I had a bad feeling in my gut, which was why I called Tex. I was stupid. I shouldn't have let Henry goad me into it. I'm just sorry that the other woman got sucked into the situation. And I'm so sorry for you too. If I'd been smarter you wouldn't have had to go through it and be reminded of your sister."

Mozart chuckled. "You're the only person I've met who after being kidnapped and tortured, would apologize for it." Then he sobered. "Sunshine, I don't give a fuck about Hurst."

"But…"

"No, let me finish." When Summer nodded, Mozart pulled her more deeply into his arms and rested his head on top of her head.

"For most of my life I've been hunting that man. He's the reason I joined the SEAL teams. I wanted revenge for Avery. I wanted to kill him more than I wanted to serve my country, more than I really cared about rescuing people, more than anything else. It had consumed my life entirely. The only reason I was in Big Bear in the first place was because Tex told me Hurst had been there. But you know what? When we got to that cabin and revenge was in sight for me, I didn't give a damn. The *only* thing I cared about was you. I didn't see Elizabeth. I didn't see Hurst. I didn't see my teammates. I only saw *you*. I got to you as soon as I could and realized I couldn't care less what happened to that fucker. I knew my teammates would make sure he didn't get away, and that was good enough for me."

"What happened to him?"

"He won't be hurting anyone else ever again."

"Will you guys get in trouble? I'll say whatever's necessary to the police and the Navy so you don't in trouble."

Mozart could tell Summer was getting worked up and he tried to reassure her.

"No, we aren't going to get in trouble, Sunshine. Our CO knew where we were and what we were doing. The police are up at the cabin now taking photos and getting evidence. Tex has sent them everything, at least everything legal, he collected on Hurst over the years. They know he was a psycho. We won't get in trouble."

He relaxed a fraction as Summer's muscles loosened. After a beat she whispered in a voice so low, Mozart almost didn't hear her, "I was so scared."

"Aw, Sunshine."

"I know I called Tex, since you were out of the country on some mission. I tried to stay strong. I told myself that Tex would figure it out and help me, but I didn't know how."

"Tell me what you can about what happened. You have to get it out. I'm not a counselor, and that's probably what you need, but I also want you to talk to me."

"I'm scared."

"Of what? Me?"

"No. Well, kinda."

Mozart's arms loosened. Shit. She was scared of

him? He prepared to get off the bed and give Summer some space.

"No! Please. I didn't mean it that way." Summer's arms tightened around Mozart, preventing him from moving away from her. "I'm not scared of *you*. I'm scared if I tell you what happened, you'll think differently about me. That you'll think I'm weak. I don't think I'm like the other women that your friends are with. Caroline is so put together. It happened to her too, but she's so strong."

"Summer, Ice is strong because of Wolf. She was a hot mess right after it happened. Hell, give yourself a break. It hasn't even been twenty-four hours, Sunshine. And you're right, I'll probably think differently about you after you tell me." When Summer jerked in his arms and tried to pull away, Mozart was the one who held on tight and pulled his head back so he could look in her eyes. "I'll be more proud of you than I am right now. I'll think you're so much stronger than I thought you were. I'll love you even more than I do right now."

Summer could only stare at Mozart in bewilderment. "Wha…"

"Yes, I love you. I've never said that to another woman before in my life. I never believed in insta-love before you. Even I know it's nuts. Hell, I haven't even been inside you yet, but I love you. If anything had happened to you, I don't know what I would've done.

Now, tell me what happened. Give it to me. Let me help you though it." He pulled her head back down so it was resting on his chest again. "Close your eyes, I know they're hurting. Relax, you're safe in my arms, now tell me."

"Bossy," Summer teased, bringing her hand up to his face and cupping it as she lay there. She ran her thumb over his cheek, realizing that he'd been through his own hell enough times that he most likely could help her work through what had happened.

She quietly described in a monotone what had happened up until the point where Hurst had taped her eyes open. Her voice broke. "He wanted me to watch. I just couldn't anymore. He got pissed and told me he'd make it so I didn't have a choice. I didn't want to see it. He might have forced my eyes open, but I refused to *see*. I thought about you. Your touch, your words, how it sounded when you called me 'Sunshine.' My eyes burned, they were so dry. The tape was pulling on my hair."

Mozart couldn't help it. "Shhhhh, Sunshine. I've got you. You're okay."

"When the bright light went off, I thought I'd been blinded. I was so scared."

"I'm so sorry…"

"No, you don't understand. When I was finally able to see again, the first thing I saw was *you*. You were blocking everything else out. I thought I was still dreaming at first. Then you were wanting to touch me, and I didn't want his filth on you. You're everything that's good and clean. I didn't want that touching you."

"Sunshine, I love that you feel that about me. But I'm not clean."

"You *are*. You've made me feel things I haven't felt in all my life. When you're around, I forget everything else. I called Tex knowing he'd find you. Somehow, no matter how crazy it was, I knew you'd come for me. You said you'd always come for me."

"Fuck, Sunshine. You're right. I'll always come for you. But please, Jesus, please, don't get in a car with a psychotic serial killer who wants to taunt me with you again."

Mozart closed his eyes when he heard Summer giggle. How the hell she could laugh after everything she'd been through, was beyond him.

"Are there any more psychotic serial killers out there who will want to kidnap me just to taunt you?"

"Fuck no."

"Then okay, I won't get in a car with any again." Summer brought her head up and looked at Mozart seriously. "I love you, Sam Reed."

"Thank God." Mozart crushed Summer to his chest again, just as a nurse entered the room.

"What do you think you're doing? You aren't allowed on the patient's bed."

Mozart didn't even twitch. He wasn't moving.

"Sir? Did you hear me?"

"Yeah, I heard you, I'm just ignoring you."

"You can't ignore me. I'll call security!"

Mozart felt Summer try to get up, and knew he had to say something to appease the shrew of a nurse before it further upset Summer.

He picked his head up off the pillow while still holding Summer tightly to him. Mozart looked at the nurse and calmly stated, "My woman has been kidnapped and tortured by a serial killer hell bent on destroying me. She just spent the last thirty minutes telling me about how that sick fuck tortured her by taping her damn eyes open and jacking off on her. I don't give a flying fuck if it's against the rules of this hospital, but I wasn't going to let her go through that without feeling safe in my arms. I'm sorry if you have a problem with that, but I'm not moving until I'm sure she's okay and is comfortable with me getting up off this bed."

Mozart put his head back down on the pillow and waited for the explosion he figured was coming. He hadn't exactly been diplomatic.

"Uh, okay, I'll just come back in a bit then."

Summer and Mozart listened as the door opened and then shut again. Summer broke the silence by giggling again. "Uh, was that really necessary?"

"Yes." Mozart wasn't ready to let it go.

"I love you, Mozart. I don't think our life will be easy and calm."

"Yes it will. I can't handle anything like this again. Oh and you should know, Ice is arranging to have all your things moved from Big Bear down to my apartment. She's also been given carte blanche to get you anything else she thinks you need that she doesn't see in your stuff. And I have to warn you, Sunshine, most likely you'll have a shit-ton of new clothes and shoes when we get home."

Not knowing what to expect from his announcement, Mozart tensed. He knew Summer was independent and didn't like it when he bought her things. Telling her she was being moved into his apartment in a different city went way beyond "buying her things."

"Okay."

Mozart was floored. "Okay?" He lifted Summer's chin so he could look into her eyes.

"Okay," Summer repeated.

"You're not freaking out. Should I expect a freak out later when you're more yourself?"

"Mozart, I just went through the worst thing I've ever been through in my life. I was scared out of my mind that I'd never see you again. I was scared that Ben would rape, torture, and kill me before I'd get to tell you how much you meant to me. I didn't really even like my job all that much and was already planning on leaving after the winter was over. I'm more than happy to move down to Riverton with you. I'll stay with you as long as you'll have me."

"You're such a pain in my ass."

Summer just smiled up at him.

"Kiss me?"

"With pleasure."

Mozart turned on his side until he was over Summer. He leaned down and gently took her lips with his own. He took his time, tasting and nibbling. When he felt her tongue reach out for his, he deepened the kiss, bringing his hand up to her cheek and holding her still, as the kiss turned carnal.

Before the kiss could go any further, they heard the door open again. Mozart reluctantly lifted his head. He didn't look away from Summer's eyes but brushed his hand over her head and tucked her hair behind her ear. He kissed each eye, each eyebrow, and finally her forehead before finally turning his head to see who had entered the room.

Seeing the doctor was leaning against the door jamb, smiling, Mozart shook his head and smiled in return. He shifted until he could get his legs over the side of the bed and he stood up. He pulled the chair closer to the side of the bed and sat down, grasping Summer's hand in his own before settling down.

"Doc, it's good to see you," he drawled semi-sarcastically.

The doctor laughed and pushed himself away from the door and came toward the bed. "Yeah, I bet. But I bring good news." He looked at Summer. "You're being discharged today. Your eyes will be okay. I'm prescribing some eye drops to help with the dryness. You'll find in a few days they'll be back to normal. Your other injuries will just take some time to heal. I'm sending you home with some pain killers. You need to use them if the pain gets to be too much. Don't try to be a hero. Relax, rest, and you'll be as good as new in no time." He paused, obviously wanting to say something, but not knowing how to say it.

Finally, he just blurted it out. "I think it's also a good idea if you talked to someone about what happened. I can get some referrals if you need them."

"I've got it under control, doc." Mozart said darkly.

When it looked like the doctor was going to protest, Summer broke in. "I will. I promise. Mozart is a SEAL, there are a lot of doctors on the base I can talk to. He's going to set it up for me."

"Okay then. Good. I wish you the best of luck. I would recommend that you follow up with your personal physician when you get home to make sure everything is healing up as it should. A visit to your optometrist would also be a good move, again, just to make sure everything is okay."

"Will do," Mozart answered. "I'll get that set up for next week as well."

The doctor held out his hand to Mozart. "It was good to meet you Mr. Reed. Thank you for your service to our country. We're all better off for the job that you do." Visibly flustered, Mozart shook his hand. Summer giggled again at his discomfort. Some badass SEAL he was.

The doctor turned back to Summer and held out his hand to her. Shaking her hand, he said solemnly, "And good luck to you, Summer. You're an amazing woman and I'm glad you beat that son-of-a-bitch!"

Flushing, Summer didn't say anything.

"Go ahead and get dressed and get your things together. We'll discharge you as soon as we can. It can get crazy around here, but we know that leaving is generally people's favorite thing to do." He laughed at his own joke and turned to leave.

"Doctor?" Summer's voice sounded loud in the room.

"Yes, Summer?"

"Can you tell me how Elizabeth is doing?" A knot formed in Summer's stomach at the look on the doctor's face.

"I wish I could, doctor-patient privilege and all of that."

"Oh. Okay. I just…"

Mozart put his hand to Summer's cheek and turned her head toward him. "I'll find out for you, Sunshine."

"I just wanted her to know…"

When she didn't say anything else, Mozart prompted her to continue. "Know what?"

"That I wasn't getting off on what he was doing."

"What the fuck?" Mozart couldn't have bitten off the words if he'd tried.

Summer hurried to explain, "*He* told her that. He told her that he was torturing her because I'd asked him to. That I wanted him to."

"Sunshine, I'm sure she didn't believe him."

"But what if she did, Mozart?"

"She doesn't," the doctor spoke from beside Summer's bed. He'd walked back over and was speaking in a low voice. "She isn't doing as well as you are, Summer. She needed someone to talk to. I was there when she spoke briefly with the crisis counselor. She knows he was torturing you too. She told the counselor that she felt bad for *you*."

Summer's eyes burned with fresh tears. "Thank you for telling me."

"You're welcome. Now, get dressed and get out of my hospital." He smiled as he said it so Summer would know he was kidding with her.

Mozart waited until the door shut behind him. "Don't."

"Don't what?"

"Don't feel guilty. What he did to you was just as bad as what he did to her. You were both innocent in all of this."

"I know. I just feel…I don't know what I feel."

"Feel glad that you're not there anymore. Feel relief that he can't hurt anyone ever again. Feel happy that you're going home with me."

"I do, Mozart. I do."

"Okay then. Let's go home."

Chapter Eighteen

SUMMER SAT CROSS legged on the bed as Caroline, Alabama, and Fiona climbed on as well.

"How are you really doing, Summer?" Caroline asked somberly.

"I'm okay. Really. Thank you for giving me the name of your counselor. I thought I was doing okay talking with Mozart, but I realized I was still holding back with him because I didn't want to hurt him. And I knew every time I had a nightmare he was hurting."

"I know. I still feel that way sometimes. Having an unbiased person that you know you won't hurt if you tell them the fears and thoughts in your head is really important." Caroline patted Summer's knee.

"I'm not sure how we got so lucky, but I'll tell you this. I thank my lucky stars every day that I was kidnapped by those sex slavers," Fiona said unexpectedly.

"What the hell?" Alabama exclaimed, smacking Fiona lightly on the shoulder. "How can you say that?"

"Because if I hadn't been held hostage down there in

Mexico, I never would have met Hunter. I would still be living my boring life in El Paso."

"Yeah but..."

"No, no buts. I've spent a lot of time thinking about this. Things happen in our lives for a reason. Caroline, you were on that plane so you could smell that drugged ice. Matthew was sitting next to you so he could save everyone's lives on board. Alabama, you saved Christopher's life at that party. If you hadn't been there to lead him to safety, he might not be around today. Yes, everything you went through with him sucked, but the bottom line is that he's still around today because of you. I met Hunter as a direct result of what happened to me in Mexico. And Summer, there are so many ways to look at what happened to you, but the bottom line is that if poor little Avery hadn't been killed when she was little, you never would have met Sam, and Ben Hurst might still be out there killing people today." Fiona let her words sink in before she continued.

"We can piss and moan about our lives and the hell we each went through, but the bottom line is that we wouldn't be with our men today if our lives hadn't played out as they had. I'm dealing with my issues, and you guys are dealing with yours, but at the end of the day we get to fall asleep in the arms of our men...and I wouldn't change one minute of my life if it meant losing that."

"Wow." Summer couldn't really disagree with Fiona. She was right. It helped put everything in perspective for her in a way she knew she never would have come up with on her own. She sent up a silent prayer for Avery. She'd never get the chance to meet her, but she'd be grateful to her for the rest of her life.

When everyone was quiet for a bit, Fiona finally broke the silence. "Okay, enough of that. Caroline, get out the drinks. We need to party!"

Everyone laughed. Caroline had browbeat Matthew until he'd agreed to let her host their little get together in the basement of their house. Alabama had spent a lot of time there after she'd been arrested and Christopher had his head up his ass, and it had become the hangout place when the women wanted to get together and let loose. Their men weren't comfortable with them going out all the time, so to appease them, they let loose in the basement while the SEALs were upstairs waiting them out.

Alabama and Christopher usually crashed in the bed there in the basement, and Hunter always took Fiona home. Since this was the first time Summer had been invited, she wasn't sure what Mozart would do, but she figured he'd sweep her home as soon as she popped her head upstairs again. He'd been crazy protective, but Summer secretly loved every second of his Alpha protectiveness. She still sometimes looked over her shoulder thinking she saw Ben, but knew he was dead.

On their way home from the hospital, Mozart had explained what had happened at the cabin. Wolf had decided to bring Hurst in to face the justice system for what he'd done to not only Elizabeth and Summer, but for every woman and child he'd murdered over the years. Wolf knew every one of his teammates wanted to slit Hurst's throat for not only what he'd done to Mozart's woman and sister, but for all the women and children he'd tortured over the years. But when they'd gone to bring Hurst out of the cabin, he'd turned on Benny and tried to gut him with a knife he'd had in his pants pocket. Wolf had shot him right between the eyes and Hurst had fallen down dead.

They were all a bit pissed the man hadn't suffered more, but it had been deemed a case of self-defense. There was no way anyone was going to put a SEAL team on the stand for murder, not with Hurst's history and with the testimony of Summer and Elizabeth about what had gone on in the cabin.

Sitting in the basement of Caroline's house, drinking Sex on the Beaches, Midori Sours, and Screwdrivers, Summer never felt safer. She knew her SEAL and three others were upstairs impatiently waiting for their female bonding to be over. They might gripe and complain about it, but they all knew they'd give their women whatever they wanted.

After another two hours, the women finally took pity on the men, at least that was what they said to each other. Summer chuckled, knowing the other women enough to know they were all horny as hell and wanted nothing more than to jump their men.

Mozart hadn't wanted to rush her and they'd yet to make love, but Summer was hoping tonight was the night. She was more than ready. They'd had some pretty heavy make out sessions over the last two weeks, but she wanted more than that. She wasn't sure what Mozart was waiting for, but she was determined to break through his resolve tonight.

The women all tripped up the stairs laughing and hanging off one another. They burst through the basement door into the kitchen and laughed anew at the looks on the men's faces. Each woman stumbled over to her man.

Summer loved the smile that was on Mozart's face. He'd turned in his seat as soon as he'd seen her, and he now pulled her to stand between his legs.

"Did you have a good time, Sunshine?"

"Yeah, you have the best friends."

"They're your friends too, Summer."

"Oh yeah, *we* have the best friends." Summer beamed at Mozart.

"Oh yeah, you're ready to go." Mozart looked around at his teammates. Yeah, they were going. Wolf and Ice were oblivious to anyone around them. They were locked in each other's arms and in another five minutes would probably be going at it on the table. Abe had hauled Alabama up in his arms and was heading toward the basement door. Mozart bet they would also be more than occupied within five minutes.

He met Cookie's eyes across the table and they smiled at each other. They were the poor saps that had to drive home. It'd take them at least another half an hour before they'd be able to crawl into bed with their women.

"You have a key right? Wolf is always too occupied to bother with locking the door behind us," Mozart asked almost rhetorically.

"Yeah, I've got it. Go on, get Summer home. I've got this."

Mozart laughed. Fiona was sitting in Cookie's lap alternating between kissing his neck and sucking on his earlobe.

"God, I love girls-night-in," Cookie said, as he tilted his head to give Fiona more access.

Mozart just shook his head and looked back at Summer.

"Ready to go?"

"Yeah. I'm ready."

At the weird tone of her voice, Mozart took a hard look at Summer. She was grinning at him a little crookedly. He could tell she was tipsy, but she wasn't falling-down drunk. "What?"

"Nothing, let's go." Summer took a step back and tugged on his hand. Mozart stood up and followed her to the front door and out to his SUV.

He watched as her eyes darted from side to side as he walked around the vehicle to get into the driver's side. He hated that she still felt the need to get a sense of her surroundings. If she hadn't been through what she had with Hurst, Mozart would probably be proud of her for being safe. But seeing her do it now just pissed him off. He knew he couldn't erase all her memories of that night, but he hated seeing her scared or even uncomfortable.

Mozart climbed in and pulled on his seat belt before starting the car. He felt Summer's hand on his as it rested on the gear shift.

"I'm okay, Mozart. Promise."

He lifted her hand and kissed the back of it. "You're more than okay, Sunshine. Let's go home."

The car was silent all the way back to their apartment. Both Summer and Mozart were lost in their own thoughts. After parking the car, Mozart kissed Summer's hand again.

"Stay put, Sunshine."

Summer nodded, she knew the drill.

Mozart came around the car and opened her door.

She slid out and put her hand in his. They walked up to the second floor to the apartment. Mozart didn't let go of Summer's hand as he unlocked the door and they walked in. He paused, as he usually did and tilted his head to listen to the quiet apartment. Not hearing anything unusual, and not feeling any bad vibes, he dropped the keys on the table beside the door and shut the front door.

Summer turned in his arms and looked up at him. Mozart was always saying to her that she could tell him anything, that he wanted her to be honest with him. Well, tonight she was going to be honest. The alcohol helped a bit, but the words were all hers.

"It's time. I want you."

"Summer, you've been drinking."

"I don't care. I'm not drunk. Not even close. I feel good. I feel safe. I need you, Mozart. I need you in my arms. I need you inside me. I'm starting to feel like you don't want me that way..." Even she was surprised at the words that came out. She *had* started to feel like he might not see her in the same way as he had before she'd been kidnapped. Maybe being in Hurst's clutches was too much for him.

Almost before the last word left her mouth, Mozart's lips were covering hers. He yanked her into his arms. One arm went behind her back and up her spine, to hold her upper body to his, and the other hand slid into

229

her hair, holding her head still for his assault on her senses.

Lifting his head after making her sway in his arms he growled, "Not want you? Jesus, Sunshine, I've spent every morning since we've left the hospital jacking off in the shower. The feel of you beside me in bed, your smell on my skin in the mornings and on my sheets, watching you laugh and gain your footing back after going through what you've been through…it's almost been too much."

When Summer jerked in his arms, Mozart refused to loosen his hold. "I want you to be sure. I want you to be ready for me. I can't get inside you and then let you go. If we do this, I won't let you go."

"I don't want you to let me go."

"Are you sure you're ready for this?"

"Yes, I've never been more ready in my entire life," Summer paused a moment. "Have you really been…you know…in the shower?"

"Yes. But it doesn't help. The second I walk into the room and see you in my bed I get hard all over again."

"I do too."

"What?" Mozart didn't understand what Summer was saying.

"I do that too…in the shower…after you go to work…"

Mozart leaned down and swept Summer off her feet.

Without a word he carried her into their room and set her on her feet next to the bed.

"Clothes. Off."

Smirking at his lapse into caveman speak, Summer slowly pulled her shirt over her head. She watched as Mozart's eyes widened and he stood stock still, his hands motionless on the button of his jeans. Enjoying the fact that her striptease was rendering him immobile, Summer reached down and pulled off her tennis shoes one at a time, bending low so he could see her cleavage. She toed off her socks next and then loosened her jeans.

Wanting to spur Mozart into action, Summer asked cheekily, "Am I the only one that's gonna be naked tonight?"

"Fuck no." Mozart finally jerked into action. He whipped his shirt over his head and let it fall behind him without a thought. He then ripped open the button on his jeans and jerked them down his legs.

Summer grinned and eased her own jeans down her legs. Finally, they stood staring at each other in nothing but their underwear. Summer could feel her own wetness; she shuffled her feet. She could see Mozart was excited too. He certainly was big, she could see the outline of his manhood clearly through his cotton briefs. She reached behind her and unhooked her bra. She let it fall off her arms to drop at her feet. That apparently was enough to push Mozart into motion.

As Mozart took a step toward her, she stepped back. Finally, he was almost touching her and Summer could feel the bed at the back of her knees. With one more step, she sat hard on the edge of the mattress. Mozart went to his knees in front of her. He grabbed the side of her panties and growled, "Lift up."

Summer lifted her hips so Mozart could peel her undies down her legs. He wasted no time and as soon as the scrap of cotton cleared her ankles, he was up and pushing her back on the bed with a hand to her chest.

"Scoot back." As Summer scrambled to move backward on the bed, Mozart ripped his briefs off and then came up onto the bed and over Summer. He crawled on his hands and knees over her as she wiggled her way up the bed.

Satisfied with her location, Mozart dropped his hips onto hers and pressed down. Summer could feel his length against her heat and stomach.

"I want to go slow, but I'm not sure I can." Mozart put his forehead on hers and took a deep breath. "You can't touch me. If this is going to work, you can't touch me."

"Screw that!" Summer returned immediately. She brought her hand up to his scarred cheek. "Mozart, we have all the time in the world. I don't care if our first time lasts five minutes or five hours, because I know after the first time, there'll be a second. After the second, there'll be a third. After the third, there'll be a fourth. Eventually we'll make it to the shower and we can do to each other what we've been doing to ourselves. There aren't a ton of rooms in this apartment, but you do have quite a bit of furniture that I'm sure we can get creative on. Don't you get it, Mozart? I'm happy to just be here with you. I want to touch you and have you touch me back. Don't overthink it."

Mozart laughed. Summer was right. "You're right." He reared back a fraction then slowly brought his hips back down to hers and entered her at the same time. They both groaned. "Is this okay? Shit, tell me this is all right!"

"It's wonderful. Fantastic. If you stop I'll have to hurt you!" Summer put her hands on Mozart's butt and pulled him the last few inches until he rested against her as close as he could get. They both groaned.

"When we met, you bragged that I'd made you come three times before dinner...well, I can't promise that, because it's after dinner, but I can promise you those three orgasms."

Summer laughed and then they both groaned again.

"I can feel you clench on me when you laugh. I've never felt anything like it." Suddenly Mozart stilled. "Oh shit. Sunshine. I can't. You have to stop."

Summer continued to clench against his length. She squeezed him with her inner muscles as hard as she could. "Don't stop, Mozart. Please don't stop."

"I'm not covered baby. I'm not protected."

"I don't care."

Mozart stopped moving and reared back enough so that only the tip of his hardness was inside her. "Sunshine, are you on the pill?"

"No, but I was on the shot. I know it's not good forever, but I think it's still okay."

"I'm not willing to take a chance on a 'think.'"

Tears filled Summer's eyes, and Mozart leaned down and kissed them away.

"Don't cry, Jesus, don't cry."

"You don't want a baby with me?"

"I want *you*, Summer. If we decide down the line that a baby is what we want, we'll plan for it and make a baby with intent. For now? No, I don't want a baby. I just want you. I want to spend time getting to know *you*. I want to be able to go out to dinner and not worry about our child. I want to take trips with you. I don't want to leave you and a child while I go out on missions."

Summer took a deep breath. He was right. She wasn't ready for a baby either. "I want our first time to be just us. No latex."

Mozart took a deep breath. "I'm clean, I swear. I know I've been with way too many women in the past, but that was in the past. I haven't been with anyone since I met you. I get tested by the Navy."

"Okay, Mozart. I'm clean too."

Mozart laughed, Summer thinking she wasn't clean was almost a joke. Of course she was. "Of course you are, Sunshine. Okay, birth control. When was your last period?" Mozart laughed when Summer blushed. "Sunshine, you talk to me about other things, this shouldn't be embarrassing."

"But it is."

Mozart pushed inside Summer slowly and relentlessly until he couldn't get inside her anymore, then pulled out so that she only had his tip again. "Tell me."

"Bossy," but Summer said it with a smile. "I'm due to start in a few days."

"It should be safe. I'll pull out, if it won't bring back too many bad memories for you." Mozart couldn't help but think about what Hurst had done to her in the cabin.

"It's fine. It's not the same at all. I want to see you, feel you in me, but Mozart, there's still a risk." Summer smiled so Mozart would know she wasn't upset at him.

At her smile, Mozart grinned back. "I know it's not foolproof, but it's better than nothing. And you're right, I want our first time to be just us, with nothing between us. Now, lie back and let me concentrate, woman."

Summer giggled again and smiled as Mozart groaned. Her giggles quickly turned to moans as he pushed inside her again. All thought of laughing quickly left her mind as Mozart set about driving her crazy. It wasn't until Summer had climaxed a second time that Mozart began to thrust into her harder.

"Yes, baby, that's it. Take me. I'm yours."

Her words pushed Mozart over the edge. He pulled out quickly and started to release on Summer's stomach. He was floored when he felt her soft, little hand stroking him and coaxing more of his cum from his manhood. He watched as Summer used one hand to caress his softening length and the other to rub his release into her skin.

"Jesus. You're killing me, Sunshine."

"I love the feel of you on me."

Mozart lowered himself onto Summer. She brought her arms up in between them and Mozart could feel his wetness on her fingertips as she caressed his chest.

"I love you."

"I love you too."

They lay on the bed for a few minutes before Summer broke the silence. "I'll go to the doctor soon and start on the shot again."

"Okay, Sunshine."

"I want to feel you fill me up."

"*Yes*. I want that too."

Mozart peeled himself off Summer's chest and he smiled as she giggled once again.

"Uh, I think we need a shower."

"I recall you saying that when we first met too. Didn't you promise me 'one more round in the shower'?"

"I'm never going to live that down am I?"

"It was the best day of my life, Sunshine. I hope neither of us ever forget it."

"Me either."

"Let's go rock each other's world."

Summer smiled and took the hand Mozart held out to her as he stood by the side of the bed. She thought back to what Fiona had said earlier that night. Things happen in our lives for a reason. While being kidnapped and tortured by Ben Hurst hadn't been fun, it was a part of her being able to be where she was right now. Summer loved Mozart so much she couldn't imagine her life without him.

She took Mozart's hand and smiled all the way to the bathroom, ready to rock his world and to have hers rocked in return.

Epilogue

T HE TEAM SAT around the table at *Aces Bar and Grill* enjoying each other's company and ribbing each other good naturedly.

Jess, their usual waitress, put down a round of beers.

"Here you go, guys."

"Thanks, Jess. Hey, you got your hair cut," Benny said.

Jess looked up in surprise at the good looking group of men, locking eyes with Benny.

"Uh yeah, it was...uh...always in my face." Jess nervously smoothed a stray lock of hair behind her ear.

"Hmm, I guess I've never see it down, you've always had it pulled back when we've seen you here."

"Yeah, well, I needed a change."

Hearing the bartender calling her name, Jess looked over and saw the bartender gesturing at her. She turned back to the table. "I'll be back in a bit to see if you guys need anything else." She then turned and limped over to the bar to pick up another order to deliver.

Dude brought up the subject they were talking about before their drinks arrived. "As I was saying, you guys are pathetic!" He rolled his eyes at the men sitting around the table. "Seriously, you never want to go out anymore, you stay home all the time. You're all a bunch of fuddy duddies now that you have women."

"Hey, you're just jealous," Mozart shot back, laughing at his friend.

Dude wouldn't admit it, but he knew Mozart wasn't exactly wrong. He'd never really thought about settling down until he'd watched his friends find women to love one by one. And the women they'd found were awesome. He didn't like that they'd had to rescue Ice, Fiona, and Summer from awful situations, but he was pleased as all get out that they were now safe and with his friends.

Because most of their team was married now, the CO had backed off sending them on some of the more extreme missions they'd been on in the beginning of their careers. And both Dude and Benny were okay with that. They weren't as young as they used to be and the last thing any of them wanted to do was come home and have to tell one of their women that they'd lost their SEAL.

But Dude wasn't sure where he was supposed to find a woman of the caliber of his teammates'. He knew he wasn't the best candidate for a woman. He was too stubborn and needed too much control in his life. He tried not to let it bother him, but every time he saw Ice run her fingers down Wolf's face and laugh when she felt his stubble on her skin, or when he'd watch Fiona run her hand over Cookie's head, Dude knew in his gut he most likely wouldn't ever have that.

His left hand was too badly scarred, too mangled, too ugly to have a woman really take him seriously. He'd seen it time and time again. He'd meet a good looking woman while out at the bars and they'd be hitting it off, but when they saw his left hand they'd always back off.

He looked down at his hand. He was missing parts of three fingers that were blown off by the toe-popper on one of their missions. He was actually lucky it had been his left hand, and even more lucky to have only lost part of his fingers. He could still be a SEAL and he could still work with explosives, but it'd really put a crimp on his love life.

His wants in the bedroom was another reason Dude figured he'd never find a woman to settle down with permanently. It was one thing for a woman to want to play in the bedroom with him for a while, but another to accept the way he was full time. It was a novelty for a few nights to be told what to do and how to do it while in his bed, Dude had learned that more than that, women just plain didn't want long term.

Dude mentally shrugged. The hell with it.

The men were startled when Wolf's cell phone rang. They watched as he answered it and they all sat up straighter when they saw his muscles get tight.

"Right, yeah, I'll get him on it. Thanks." Wolf hung up the phone and turned to Dude.

"Bomb threat at the big grocery store on Main Street. They're asking for an ordinance expert."

"I'm on it." Dude stood up quickly, already thinking about what he might find. The local police department would sometimes call on the military when they needed extra help. This apparently was one of the times when they felt like the extra help would be needed.

"Be safe. Let us know if you need anything."

Dude raised his hand in acknowledgement of Wolf's words, then he was gone.

Look for the next book in the
SEAL of Protection Series:
Protecting Cheyenne.

Discover other titles by Susan Stoker

Badge of Honor: Texas Heroes Series
Justice for Mackenzie
Justice for Mickie
Justice for Corrie
Justice for Laine (novella)
Shelter for Elizabeth
Justice for Boone
Shelter for Adeline (TBA)
Justice for Sidney (TBA)
Shelter for Blythe (TBA)
Justice for Milena (TBA)
Shelter for Sophie (TBA)
Justice for Kinley (TBA)
Shelter for Promise (TBA)
Shelter for Koren (TBA)
Shelter for Penelope (TBA)

Beyond Reality Series
Outback Hearts
Flaming Hearts
Frozen Hearts

Writing as Annie George
Stepbrother Virgin (erotic novella)

Connect with Susan Online

Susan's Facebook Profile and Page:
www.facebook.com/authorsstoker
www.facebook.com/authorsusanstoker

Follow Susan on Twitter:
www.twitter.com/Susan_Stoker

Find Susan's Books on Goodreads:
www.goodreads.com/SusanStoker

Email: Susan@StokerAces.com

Website: www.StokerAces.com

To sign up for Susan's Newsletter go to:
http://bit.ly/SusanStokerNewsletter

Or text: STOKER to 24587 for text alerts on your mobile device

About the Author

New York Times, USA Today, and *Wall Street Journal* Bestselling Author Susan Stoker has a heart as big as the state of Texas, where she lives, but this all-American girl has also spent the last fourteen years living in Missouri, California, Colorado, and Indiana. She's married to a retired Army man who now gets to follow *her* around the country.

She debuted her first series in 2014 and quickly followed that up with the SEAL of Protection Series, which solidified her love of writing and creating stories readers can get lost in.

If you enjoyed this book, or any book, please consider leaving a review. It's appreciated by authors more than you'll know.

CPSIA information can be obtained
at www.ICGtesting.com
Printed in the USA
LVHW050541210820
663773LV00022B/2688